CATASTROPHE IN THE LIBRARY

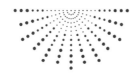

CEECEE JAMES

For my Family — I love you guys soo much. You all are uniquely made and a treasure to me on this crazy, lovely, rollercoaster journey called life. Like Grandpa always used to say, "Keep Looking Up."

xxxxxxxxx

And to Riley Jean — May this little mystery remind you that you are a gift from God to your parents… as they are to you.

CONTENTS

CHAPTER ONE

*I*t's strange how a night can be too quiet. Tonight's silence defined spooky with an underline and a couple of exclamation points. I had no idea why it bothered me, making my skin crawl like spiders danced along my spine. I tried to ignore the feeling and climbed into bed.

I tugged the lavender-scented sheets up to my chin. Hank, my favorite marmalade cat, curled around my feet, which were now trapped by his copious weight.

I'd thought to start counting sheep when screams shattered the silence like a plate glass mirror smashing to the ground. I leaped out of bed and onto a floor that bit the soles of my feet with its iciness and ran to the door.

Wrenching it open allowed the cascade of shrieks to resonate around me, seemingly coming from every direction. I looked around, shivering and not knowing which way to turn. Other doors down the hallway banged open, and more confused, sleepy women stumbled out onto the same cold floor.

"Heaven help us! Who is it?" Cook yelled, stepping forward with the firmness of someone taking control. She wasn't having mindless screaming, not on her watch. "What's the matter?"

"A voice! I heard it! I felt a gust of air, and someone touched my arm," Janet cried from the end of the hallway. It made me shiver to see the fear on her white face.

"Who was there?" Mary demanded, her curls tied back in a scarf. Because of her short height, she had to stand on her tiptoes to see over us and into Janet's bedroom.

"Someone! Maybe a robber!" Janet sobbed, covering her chest with her arms.

A hush settled over the group as we all digested that bit of hysterical information.

"I haven't heard anyone running past my room, and it seems we would have if it just happened," Jessie declared.

I thought the same. I hadn't heard anything either, but then perhaps I'd been closer to sleep than I realized.

Cook took over. "A robber, pshaw," she scoffed. "We'd all have heard him come down the stairs. There's only one way out."

"Unless he was a ghost," whispered Jessie, amending her first thought. The girls around her broke into nervous whispers.

"*Unless* it was someone who went into the secret wall," I said, crossing my arms in a very practical way. After my short employment here, I'd already had enough malarky about ghosts to last me a lifetime.

"Unless it was her imagination," someone else muttered snarkily. I couldn't tell who it was.

"I know what I felt," Janet whimpered back.

Cook's tone sharpened. "You missing anything?"

The poor girl rubbed her arms as if to scrub the touch away. "I'm not sure. I ran straight out here for help."

Cook gave a firm nod. "Well, no time like the present. Let's go." Her wide hips swung, and her lips pressed together matter-of-factly as she marched into Janet's room and flipped on the switch.

I gasped at the sight. The whole room had been tossed like it had been inside a clothes dryer. Not one square inch remained untouched.

Cook's eyebrows shot up. "You're right! Someone's chucked the place real good. Good gracious, girl, you didn't hear that happening?"

Janet blushed, her cheeks glowing under the ceiling light. "Actually, I've been meaning to clean it. It got a little out of hand. I've just been busy."

"Busy?" Cook blinked. As someone who demanded the kitchen be cleaned within an inch of its life, it was easy to see Janet's excuse didn't compute.

"Sometimes that happens. You should see my sister's place." Mary rushed in to defend Janet. As usual, Mary always knew the right thing to say. Made me glad we were such good friends.

Cook's eyelids fluttered closed, but she didn't respond. Gingerly, she stepped over a pile of laundry. "You should take that down to the washing machine."

Janet smiled nervously. "Actually, that's my clean clothes. The dirty stuff is over there." She pointed at a pile.

Sure enough, a mountain of clothing looked kicked to the corner.

Cook stopped in midstep. Apparently, she didn't want to intrude further. "Well, check around, dearie. I suppose you're the only one to know if something is missing."

Janet walked into the room. It was like watching someone in an Easter egg hunt all by themselves. She pushed piles over, pulled back covers, moved a stack of books.

She lingered near her dresser. It appeared in the same disarray as the rest of the room, but something about the odd pile of makeup, socks, and stacks of books caused her to frown. She picked up a handkerchief, moved a shirt, and gasped.

"What is it?" Cook moved closer, and I followed. The whole room heated up with all of us in here.

"It's my lucky ring! It's gone!"

"There's no way you could know that," Jessie scoffed. "I saw you twirling it in your hand the other day. You probably took it off and left it in the kitchen."

"I did *not* leave it downstairs," Janet spoke indignantly.

Cook waved her hands at us to shoo us away. "This is getting us nowhere. Let's get back to bed. Patty will be here squawking like a peed-on chicken any moment, and we don't want to deal with that."

The name *Patty* sobered us like a pail of cold water. Half the group scattered back to their rooms before Cook said another word.

"Someone was in here!" Janet insisted. "You guys don't care."

"Well, they're not here now. Shut your door tight and go to bed. We'll deal with this in the morning." Cook marched away.

I started to my room but hesitated. Janet looked so alone and scared. "You want to sleep in my room tonight?" I asked.

She shook her head. "Thanks, Laura Lee, but no. Besides, that person might show up in your room next."

With those chilling words, she shut the door. It didn't feel good to be left alone in the cold hallway. Shivering, I hurried back to mine.

THE NEXT MORNING, nervous energy filled our breakfast chores. As gossip often does, stories about the night's adventure twisted its weedy vines through the excited chatter all throughout the day. In the end, Patty did hear about it and brought the news straight to Miss Janice.

Cook, of course, pouted because she felt the responsibility fell to her to be the one to make the decision about whether or not the danger was real enough to bother the mistress.

Miss Janice came to the same conclusion that I had and further distrusted the hidden passageways inside the walls. Of course the police were not an option. She was horrified at the thought of strangers traipsing through the old manor's inner workings, civil workers or not.

From the first she'd heard of the secret tunnels, she'd been horrified. And then curiosity took over. I'd bring her morning coffee and catch her staring at the far wall with her eyes soft and unfocused and nose wrinkled with suspicion. Or I'd carry in the lunch tray and find her with a magazine long forgotten in her hand as she studied the wainscoting.

"Where do you suppose it all comes out at?" she'd asked me one time.

"I'm not sure." I shrugged. I'd only explored a short bit myself during one horrible adventure and found the area dirty and distasteful.

Now Miss Janice asked for volunteers to investigate them and make sure no one from Janet's scary night could come in again. Cook took one gander at the narrow gap in the bottom cupboard of the study and crossed her arms, her head shaking and bun quivering. "There's no way my behind will fit through that tiny hole. No ma'am. And I'm not one who will be stuck in the wall until eternity."

Jessie didn't even pretend to volunteer. "There's places humans don't belong, and that's one of them," she said adamantly. "Besides, that's a good way to run straight up into a ghostie." She made the sign of the cross.

So Miss Janice approached me, knowing I'd been in there before. She also roped in Stephen, her gardener, along with me. Mary's curiosity to see the end of the tunnel spurred her to volunteer. And then our good friend, Lucy, piped in as well. She didn't want us to do something without her.

After breakfast, the four of us stood outside the cupboard under the bookcase in the library. Lucy and Mary played rock-paper-scissors to see who would go in first. I simply decided it would be me and crawled into the cramped nook. The back had broken out a while ago, and I squirmed through until I stood inside the confined tunnel.

The dusty air held a whisper of the scent of old fish, and I couldn't see worth a fig. A spider could be hanging down, getting ready to explore my hair, and I wouldn't have been the wiser until I felt its tickly feet. I lifted my hand in the darkness for the wall, only to find emptiness. My heart jumped a little, but in the next sweep, I found a stud. What would my mom say if she could see me now, sidling along through the walls of this old manor? The predicament was terrible but, oddly, energizing.

"You guys can come in," I called through the little doorway.

After a few jostling moments, the three of them made their way inside the wall with me. Stephen pressed against me, trying to find room. I stumbled back while he tried to apologize.

"How can you see anything?" Lucy asked, her voice betraying her claustrophobia with a squeak.

"Hang on. Flashlight's not working," Stephen mumbled. I heard smacking against his hand, and then the light sputtered to life. "Ah, there you all are." He grinned as he swept the beam over our faces.

I squinted, and Mary squawked in protest. Lucy clutched Stephen's arm, smiling in relief for the light.

"What are we looking for?" Mary asked.

"Signs of disturbance?" I suggested.

"You don't think anyone really came in through here, do you? And went up to Janet's room?" Lucy asked.

I shrugged. "She seems to think so."

"I bet she had a bad dream and ran into the bedpost. Did you see her room?" Lucy retorted.

"Come on. Let's go," Stephen said and stepped forward. Fallen plaster popped under his shoes.

The walls pressed against us as we followed each other like a little train. Stephen shuffled around a corner, and we followed, our shoulders nearly touching the lath plaster walls. Mary stifled a sneeze at the dust.

The cold fish smell swept over me again, and I covered my nose with my shirt. "The odor doesn't get any better," I warned them.

Mary copied me, and after a second so did Lucy. Only Stephen braved the stinky air. Lucy's pupils were like two chunks of coal. I could read regret in them as she gripped Stephen's sleeve.

"You want to head back?" he asked her.

She shook her head.

"Okay, then, let's see where this bad boy ends." He reached overhead to sweep a spider web out of the way. I shivered to see it dangle from his fingers. Carefully, we followed him, all watching our steps in the narrow walkway covered in chunks of debris.

The light beam illuminated an intersection up ahead. I tried to think where we were in relation to the inside of the house, but after the second turn, I was hopelessly lost.

Stephen stopped, and we bumped to a halt behind him. He moved the light in both directions. "Left or right, ladies?"

"What was that?" Lucy squealed. She looked behind us. Her eyes widened with terror. I didn't hear anything, but that didn't keep me from spinning around.

There was nothing.

Stephen slowly flashed the beam down the tunnel. It caught two green globes that seemed to glow with their own light.

Lucy grabbed my arm in a pinch and started breathing like a farm animal. The globes blinked at us, and then the beam picked out a shock of fluffy orange. Hank fully entered into the light, a cobweb hanging off his whiskers.

"Hank!" I half-screamed. "What are you doing here?"

He blinked disdainful cat eyes as if asking us the same thing.

"That darn cat," Lucy muttered, covering her face. Her arm trembled.

"You guys have to chill out, seriously," Stephen said. "We're fine. It's just an old house. Lucy, you're getting yourself worked up for nothing. And you two have already been in here." He addressed this last sentence to Mary and me.

"We haven't been this far," I said, nodding to the path on the right. "I have no idea where that goes."

"All right then. I say that's where we explore. All in favor?"

Mary and I said yes, while Lucy stared with her forehead wrinkled with definite signs of uncertainty.

"I don't want you to be scared," I told her. "If you want, I'll walk you out. Being in here isn't for everyone."

She jerked then and glanced down. Hank rubbed his head hard against her ankle. A relieved chuckle gushed out of her. "No, I'm fine. This is good for me."

Stephen made a mark on the dirt in the intersection, and we continued on. The cat followed us.

"Hank, go back. Be careful," I warned the handsome cat. He ignored me.

The tunnel twisted and turned. My throat tickled from the dust. Behind me, Mary coughed softly.

"No one's been in here," Mary said. "We would have seen their footprints in all this dust.

"Where did this dust come from anyway?" Lucy complained.

It was horrid. Stirred up, it shone like mist in the bright beam.

"It's pretty bad here," Stephen agreed.

Oddly, the farther we went, the higher the temperature rose. I heard a gurgle and stared up. Stephen did the same with the flashlight.

Rusty pipes snaked overhead. One had a slow drip, just enough to cause white to calcify on the outside and leave a pit below it.

"Water pipes. That's probably for hot water," Stephen explained.

"How do you know?"

"These come from the manor's boiler. This place is heated with steam."

I wished I hadn't known that. The temperature rose fifty degrees just with his words.

Suddenly a loud crash came somewhere behind us. We all about jumped out of our skin. Then we heard voices. The three of us stopped, softly bumping into one another.

Cook's voice came through the wall, muffled but still full of pomp and vinegar. "You don't say!"

Butler answered her. With his deep timbre, I could only make out every other word, but the gist was something he'd overheard Patty say to Marguerite.

"That woman. I have no doubt. Well, how did Marguerite respond?" Cook asked with obvious interest.

Butler said, "She wasn't happy. I can tell you that much."

"Wasn't happy, how? What did she say?"

"That was weeks ago, woman! You can't expect me to remember everything."

Exasperation drained Cook's voice of excitement. "It baffles me how bad you are at gossip."

Mary covered her mouth to stifle her laughter. Even Stephen's lip quirked up a bit. He waved us forward, and we tip-toed past the unsuspecting couple.

After another hundred feet, the tunnel came to a dead stop, ending in a wall.

"What's happening?" Mary asked. She wiped sweat from her forehead, leaving a muddy streak.

"I'm not sure. If that's the kitchen, then this,"—he turned back around—"should be the butler's pantry."

I studied the wall. Something about the boards appeared out of place. "This can't be original."

Stephen felt the wood, his fingers flexing.

"What's this weird yellow band down there?" Mary pointed. "It looks like the board had been used on something else."

I nodded, squatting to my heels to examine it. "There's a couple of rust holes that might have once held nails."

Stephen tested the board. It creaked as he pulled on it. "Not to mention there's no lath and plaster."

His gaze caught mine, and I saw a very serious question there.

"You want to do it?" I asked.

"I think we should." Sweat trickled down his face.

"What about if we find a giant rats' nest back there?" Lucy whispered.

"Maybe it's treasure," Mary added. "You know, like how Laura Lee and I found the crown."

That idea perked everyone up, even Lucy.

CATASTROPHE IN THE LIBRARY

Lucy nodded. "All right. Do it," she encouraged Stephen.

He grinned at her sudden spunkiness. "You sure?" he teased.

"Do it! Destroy the wall."

"Okay." He glanced around for something he could use as a pry bar and found an old brick. "Maybe this is what the guy used to pound in the nails on the boards." He grinned at us again. "All right, ladies. It's game on."

When the board didn't come free at his first tug, he smacked it twice with the brick and then wedged his booted foot there as a brace. His face turned red, and he grunted.

Crack! The board came off with a cloud of dust. The three of us coughed and waved the thick air. Undaunted, Stephen grabbed the next board. This one came off easier.

He stared inside the hole. His eyebrows lowered with a curious expression in the flashlight's beam. "What is that?"

We all leaned in to look.

Lucy screamed.

We didn't blame her one bit. I don't think any of us expected to see someone staring back at us with two black holes for eyes.

CHAPTER TWO

*L*ucy's continued shrieks ripped through the air, sounding straight out of a slasher film. Her arms flailed and smacked into the walls, sending up clouds of plaster as she stumbled back into Mary. My ears buzzed from the high pitch. Much to my relief, Mary wasn't having it and clapped her hand over Lucy's mouth.

"Hush, it's okay," Mary whispered and released her when she saw Lucy take a breath.

But the skeleton staring back at us said otherwise.

Stephen poked his finger into his ear and shook his head. Lucy sure had a pair of leather lungs. Slowly, the buzzing in my ears dissipated as Mary spun Lucy away from the skeleton and in the process tromped all over my feet. I pressed against the wall to give them room.

Then we heard voices on the other side of the wall. "Good heavens! I told you they'd stir up the ghosts!" yelled Cook.

"I think it's our crew!" Butler boomed back. And then I heard, "Laura Lee! Is that you?"

"Y-yes," my voice wavered. I felt sick to my stomach at what was in front of us. Even more disturbing was the long trek back to get out of there.

Stephen broke off the last board. He stepped inside the cubby and stared down at the skeleton. Shaking his head, he turned to knock on the far wall.

"I think this is the back porch." His eyebrows rumpled together. "Poor guy."

"What happened? You think he got somehow trapped in here?" I asked.

Stephen lowered to his heels to get a better look. "See that right there? The glass bottle? Maybe it fell from someplace and bashed this poor guy's head in."

His words made me feel all swoony and not in a good way. It apparently caused Lucy the same sensation because animal-like whimpers fluttered out of her throat at a regular rate.

Mary patted her hand. "Breathe through your nose. Slow and easy."

I took that advice as well.

Stephen found a nail and used it to lift a flap of the skeleton's clothing. He slid his phone from his pocket and focused on taking a picture.

"What are you looking at?" I asked, breathing through my teeth.

"It's a pocket watch. Check out that etching." He leaned back on his heels, studying the golden object. "Did you notice these clothes are pretty old-fashioned? I'd say this poor guy has been down here a long while."

"Maybe he was one of the original builders of the house?" Mary asked, crossing her arms before her as if she were cold.

Stephen shrugged. "Hard to say, really. But that watch appears expensive. Like real gold. Hard to imagine a day laborer owning something spendy like that."

"How did the bottle get down here? And how could it kill someone?" Lucy asked.

He touched the neck of the bottle with his nail. "It's got a heavy bottom."

"Maybe someone smacked him?" I asked. Wooziness ensued again.

He frowned. I appreciated the introspective expression on his face as he considered the ramifications of what I meant.

"Mary, is she saying what I think she's saying?" Lucy asked, pale-faced.

Mary swallowed and took a step toward the skeleton. She leaned over to look. "Poor sucker had an enemy down here, that's what."

Stephen flashed the light onto the skeleton's skull and grimly nodded. "I think you're right. See that crack? Caught it right there. Poor guy." He demonstrated by punching his other hand.

"I want to go, now," Lucy whispered, her thin hands plucking at Stephen's arm.

"Laura Lee, you okay?" Cook shouted through the wall. I could picture her plump face pressed against the paint.

I turned in her direction and took a deep breath. "We need to leave."

Stephen reached to press against the outer wall where he'd knocked earlier. It looked like the wall flexed even as I heard a crack. "The boards are rotten here. You think I should just break them down?"

"Do it, Stephen!" Lucy demanded. I had to admit her lips were a little green. "I can't take it another second. I wish I'd never come in here."

Stephen quickly nodded. "Right. Step back, ladies." With that, he hefted a thick-soled boot and sent his foot crashing through the board.

The dry rot made the boards split apart like cardboard. Stephen reached past the skeleton, making Lucy groan, and pulled the remaining few chunks free. The wood popped off sounding like chunks of styrofoam.

He stared back at us, his hair sweaty and hanging in his eyes. "Come on. Let's get you guys out of here."

Lucy grabbed his hand and allowed him to drag her outside. I felt terrible to see how scared she was.

Mary turned to me. "You first?"

I looked behind through the dim light filtering in from the cracked wall. "Wait, where is he?"

"Where is who?"

"Hank."

"Who cares." She rolled her eyes, exasperated. "Let's get out of here."

"You go ahead," I said and took a few steps back into the tunnel.

She stared at me to be sure I was serious and then reached for Stephen's hand for balance. In the next instant, she disappeared through the hole.

Stephen turned to me. "Ready?'

"I don't know. I can't find Hank."

"That cat knows how to take care of himself."

"Maybe. Or maybe he's never been down this way before. I can't leave him. What if he doesn't know his way back?" Instead of waiting for his answer, I stumbled back the way we came. "Hank!" I called.

"For crying out loud, Laura Lee. I swear he'll be okay."

Stephen could say what he liked. But he didn't know how worry rippled through my body every time I tried to sleep, and Hank wasn't on my bed at night. I wasn't leaving until I found that cat.

"I'll be right back, I promise." I fumbled out my phone and flashed the light forward.

"Oh for—" His words dropped to an incoherent grumble. I was encouraged, however, to hear the man's lumbering steps as he chose to follow me.

I swung the beam along the floor. Dust carpeted the boards and curled their fur over all the nails. I kept my eye out for the cat's prints with his little extra toe, passing across the bricks. I walked back to the last turn we took.

"Ah! Found them!" I exclaimed in excitement.

"You found him?" Stephen coughed.

"No, I found his footprints."

"Terrific," he deadpanned.

"Hank!" I called. The prints led in a new direction we hadn't taken. The walls were narrower here, and the path felt barely wide enough for my shoulders. Within the next few feet, it tightened even more, the crumbly walls making me claustrophobic. I couldn't turn around.

"Hank!" I called, trying to focus on relaxing. "Here, kitty, kitty, kitty."

There was no answering meow. I had to turn sideways now to get through. I flashed the beam ahead as I minced forward after the paw prints.

"This is crazy," Stephen said behind me, breathing hard. I felt sorry for him. If it was tight for me, I couldn't imagine what it was like for a broad-shouldered, athletic guy like him.

Then I heard it—a little rusty meow.

"Hank?" I called, relief flooding my voice. "He's up ahead," I said over my shoulder to Stephen.

My ankle turned on a piece of broken plaster. A painful shudder ripped through me, and I lunged for the wall. The lath shivered under my weight and sent down a shower of fresh dust.

"You okay?" I felt Stephen's hand on my elbow.

I nodded. It was a lie, but I was going to make it true.

"That cat is completely oblivious that he's in trouble. He's not trying to come to us," he grumbled.

I would have responded, but Hank meowed louder.

"He needs me to find him for some reason." The space was tighter than ever, but I scraped through.

"You sure about this?" Stephen asked.

I ignored him and also ignored how the walls lath now pressed against my back and stomach.

"I don't know how much further I can go," Stephen confessed. "And I really don't feel comfortable with you going by yourself. What if something falls on you?"

It turned out that was the least of our worries.

CHAPTER THREE

"*H*ank!" I gasped, waving my hand at the rising dust. I coughed. "Where are you, buddy?"

I heard a rusty meow. Hank answered me again, and he never did that. Then I remembered the crash we'd heard earlier that had scared Lucy, and my heart sped up. What if something had fallen on him, and he was hurt? I shoved forward as the walls narrowed even more, ignoring the plaster scratching at my clothing and clawing into my arms. With the final four squirming feet, I spotted the orange cat.

"I see him," I gasped in relief back to Stephen.

Hank sat in the corner and blinked as the beam from the flashlight swept over his face. Casually he washed his ear. I felt like an idiot. Obviously he was fine, like Stephen had said.

Then I saw the cat was sitting on something. "What's that?"

I leaned down to pick it up, which made him give me a sassy meow. It was a leather envelope.

"You got him, Laura Lee?"

I turned the thin package over in my hand, but the griminess made it impossible to know what it was. I spotted a spider sliding down its silk from the ceiling, and I no longer cared about anything other than getting out of there. Scooping Hank to my shoulder, I answered, "I'm coming!" Slowly, I squeezed my way back.

Stephen wiped off his face with his forearm. I realized my shirt was sticking to me as well. He grunted, pleased to see Hank, and we made our way back to the wall he'd busted through. Finally, Stephen slithered through the hole and then reached through to help me out. I hated stepping over the skeleton and buried my face in Hank's fur so I couldn't see.

The cool air greeted me and made me a bit teary with relief. Both Mary and Lucy waited outside with dust-streaked faces, looking every bit like bedraggled chimney sweeps.

"What took you so long?" Mary demanded crossly. She glanced at my hand. "And what's that?"

"I'm not sure. Something Hank found."

Lucy picked a cobweb out of my hair. She did the heebie-jeebie dance trying to get it off her finger. I brushed bits of plaster off of my shirt. All I wanted to do right now was to get in the shower and put on some clean clothes. But first, we had to tell Miss Janice about the skeleton we'd found.

She was going to flip.

Oh, how I wished Marguerite were here to soften the blow. But the head housekeeper was still on her vacation. The last three weeks had never felt so long in my life.

In the meantime, we had to deal with her temporary replacement, Patty. Patty and a skeleton. Patty who was unhappy with everything and everyone at the manor. It hardly seemed fair.

"Well, let's go rip off the band-aid." I trudged up the hill with Hank heavy in my arms. Even worse, he wanted down and was making his demands known with a few claw pricks and stiffened legs.

I left him in the pantry for Cook to care for, and then we found Miss Janice in her garden room. She sat in front of a chintz-covered table, arranging her roses in a crystal vase. She took one long stare at our group before going back to trimming a stem. "You're finally back. That took forever. I assume you have an explanation for your appearance?"

I cleared my throat. "It's really dirty inside the walls."

"No. I'm referring to the look in your eyes that says you're about to deliver bad news."

The woman was astute. But before I could get a word out, Patty rushed in. Her cheeks flushed, and she carried a tray. The teapot sloshed as she ran.

"Ma'am, your tea." She dropped the tray down so hard the kettle lid rattled on the pot.

Miss Janice's fingers froze on the rose stem. Her eyes cut over to study the tray and then up to Patty's face. "Thank you," she said dryly.

Patty glanced at me. "Oh, my goodness! Where's your uniform?" She turned to Miss Janice. "Is this girl bothering you?"

Miss Janice sighed. "That will be all, Patty. Thank you again."

Patty nodded and bobbed twice at the waist. Miss Janice's face stiffened. "Dinner will be in an hour, ma'am."

"An hour?"

"Yes, I told Cook we needed to get onto a better schedule. It's good for the digestion, you know. We can't be serving dinner after seven. Good grief, there've been times you didn't get served until eight or nine. Terrible."

Miss Janice stared at her. I've been a victim of that intense gaze, and I shivered for Patty.

27

But Patty didn't seem to know the danger she was in. After another bob which sent her short hair swinging, she scooted out from the room with a satisfied air.

Miss Janice closed her eyes for a brief moment and then picked up her cup for a small sip. She froze. Her eyes went wide like she held a cricket in her mouth. I didn't see the swallow go down.

"Are you okay?" I asked uncertainly.

Miss Janice grimaced, swallowed, and delicately wiped her mouth with the linen napkin. I swear her eyes were watering. Apparently, Patty needed some tea-making lessons. And now I had to follow that act.

I took a deep breath. "Unfortunately, we need to call the police."

"Whatever for?"

Stephen cleared his throat. "We found a skeleton under the porch."

"Under the porch?" Her voice rose several octaves.

I nodded. "And it seems the poor person may have been been murdered."

Miss Janice fanned her face. She reached for her teacup again before remembering and flinching away.

"The skeleton is very old. He may be one of the original builders," I rushed in to keep her calm.

"How extraordinary," she said, pressing her lips together, causing angry lines to whisker out. It was as if the builder had personally done something to offend her. "Very well. I'll have Butler ring for them."

I nodded gratefully, and we headed for the exit. We split up in the hallway. Stephen waved goodbye to us and left for the front door.

I'd barely made it around the corner and down the hallway when both Mary and Lucy leaped out of a doorway and grabbed my arms.

"How did that go?" Mary asked.

"As well as could be expected." I shrugged.

"We saw Patty come down the hallway and had to hide," Lucy confessed.

Mary rolled her eyes.

"She brought Miss Janice her tea. However, I don't think she made it very well," I explained. To be honest, I couldn't judge Patty too hard. There was a certain protocol Miss Janice expected for tea preparations that went past my skill set of microwaving a teabag in a cup.

Mary sighed. "This will be three days in a row that Miss Janice asks for her headache tonic early."

"And the police?" Lucy asked, bringing us back to the problem at hand.

"She's having Butler do it. They'll be here soon."

In fact, nearly an hour passed before the police arrived. By the time I'd finished my shower and returned to my vacuuming, they'd raked the place over, and the coroner showed up. The police examined the entire space under the porch and even ventured into the house tunnels a bit. Mary had already plied Miss Janice with her special tonic by the time the officers exhumed the skeleton and took him away in a body bag.

Because of Stephen, we now even had an idea of who the mysterious man was, besides Mr. Bones, as Mary had dubbed him. When he returned to the house after he cleaned up, Cook tried to fortify him with some fresh cookies and milk. I think she had a bit of a crush on him. In trade, he showed Cook the picture he'd taken of the pocket watch.

Cook took one look at it and gasped. "Why, that's Uncle Bernie's watch."

"Who's that?" Mary asked, glancing up from washing dishes. I waited with a towel to dry.

"Bernie was Mr. Thornberry's brother. You know what, come with me." Then she grabbed our arms by the elbow and hustled us into the hallway, with Stephen following.

We gave each other confused glances over her head as we hurried to keep up. A minute later, we were standing in the middle of a long row of paintings that lined the great hall. "See that portrait right there? That's Bernie Thornberry." Her eyes softened.

"Did you know him?" I asked.

The wistful expression disappeared as she briskly turned to me and nodded. "He was around when I first started working here. I was a young gal myself, back then. Not even seventeen. I swear he gave me the vapors back then."

Vapors. I covered my mouth to hide my smile.

"Wow, you've been here a long time, Cook," Mary mused.

Cook snorted. "You make it sound like I'm ancient!"

Mary quickly denied that, but it was easy to see she believed it.

I think Cook saw that too, because her chest swelled as she took in a big breath. But her retort was cut off when Patty walked down the hallway with a scowl on her face.

"What are you guys doing out here? Having a party? Shouldn't you be in the kitchen? Miss Janice mentioned the eggs were cold this morning. Perhaps do better for the next meal. And you three," she swung around to address us. "Do we need to add more chores to the daily list? It seems obvious you have time to spare."

Cook glowered but stalked back to the kitchen. Mary and Stephen scattered like crickets when a hen approaches. That left me for Patty to punish. She sent me to clean every toilet in the manor for the second time that day.

CHAPTER FOUR

here was no time for us to sneak away and talk for the rest of the day. Even though the police had left, we were all still on edge. Patty continued her rampage, fueled even further by Miss Janice's refusal of the headache tonic she'd taken great pains to make. Naturally, Patty managed to pin the blame for that on us as well, citing how we hadn't kept the bottles rotated. We did our best to stay out of her sight. After all, no one liked to clean toilets and windows for hours on end.

Janet caught my eyes as she passed by with an armload of folded towels. "Emergency book club meeting tonight at ten. Spread the word."

Patty, who seemed to be everyplace, appeared then at the other end of the hallway. Her eyes narrowed at the sight of the two of us.

I turned away to the housekeeping closet. She continued down the hallway, and I swear I felt a cold breeze as she passed.

I spent a moment organizing the cleaning supplies, stalling to give her time to get far away. Finally, I made my way back to the kitchen. It was approaching dinner time, and Cook always appreciated extra hands to help with the final preparations.

As soon as the kitchen door shut behind me, I breathed a sigh of relief. The room held the homey scent of something rich, brown, and bubbling. Finally, I could let my hair down and relax.

Patty strode out of the Butler's pantry with Mary following. I flinched. How was this woman everywhere? Mary's mouth was decidedly downturned, and her eyes showed misery.

The temporary head-housekeeper complained, "Cook, I'm not happy with your pantry. It needs professional organization. Is this how the old housekeeper allowed things?"

Cook's eyebrows flickered up at the word "old." She adjusted her glittery headband. "You know Marguerite will be back in two weeks."

Patty smirked. "Not if I have anything to do about it. Trust me, I'll show Miss Janice what she's been missing once I get this household into shape. I'll be in there tomorrow to straighten out that pantry."

Cook turned away, but not before I saw her roll her eyes.

Patty zcrocd in on me. "What are you doing, Laura Lee? Didn't I just see you upstairs?"

Luckily, I saw some fresh produce on the counter and reached for a head of lettuce for an explanation.

"She's helping me make a salad," Cook answered coolly.

Patty's eyes narrowed as her arms crossed over her chest. The silence in the kitchen grew uncomfortable. Instead of being broken by usual laughter and light gossip, the atmosphere magnified by the sounds of clanging pans, scraping spoons, and water running.

I chopped the lettuce and glanced at the clock. Mary pulled out the dinner china. Patty had to be leaving the room soon, right?

Nope. She eased out a chair and plunked down to watch us. I couldn't believe she didn't even get herself a cup of tea. Instead, she kept those tiny eyes flittering between the three of us like she was at a sporting event, and she was not pleased with the outcome.

CEECEE JAMES

We had to figure out how to notify each other about the book club. I peeled carrots and glanced over at Cook. She caught the look, winked, then fanned her fingers at me twice.

I barely nodded. Affirmation she knew about the club happening tonight at ten.

Patty reached for a magazine in the middle of the table—some gossip rag one of the girls had discarded—and pulled on a pair of glasses as if to read. However, she continued to watch us, her eyes squinting in an angry-wrinkled way. Finally, she demanded, "Where is the first course for the missus?"

"It's right here," Cook said and pointed to a tureen that Janet tidied with a napkin.

"My goodness, what a production. And you're late already. Get that out there, and for Pete's sake put on a clean apron!" She shooed her fingers at Janet.

Janet rushed for an apron. As she passed Mary, Janet did the same five-flashing wave twice. At the last second, she changed the gesture into brushing a curl back from her head.

"What are you girls doing? Swatting flies?" Patty glared over her readers and then flopped the magazine open to a new page.

Now most everyone received the advanced warning about the club tonight so no one would go to sleep right away. I was surprised Patty hadn't mentioned the skeleton we'd found. It showed how much the staff truly had her frozen out.

"Where's Miss Janice eating?" Janet softly asked Cook.

Cook sniffed. "Family dining room tonight."

Her display of disdain surprised me. Normally Cook appreciated the more homey room over the audacious formal dining chamber.

Janet reached the tureen and carried it carefully through the door. Five minutes later, the door crashed against the wall as she rushed back in, her eyes wide. "Why didn't anyone tell me Miss Janice had a guest?"

"What guest does she have?" Cook frowned.

Janet spoke in an accent. "Mr. Gerald Hawkings."

I'd never met him, but whenever anyone brought up his name they spoke in that same exact way.

Patty leaped to her stubby feet, the magazine falling forgotten to the table. "Someone is here?" she wailed.

"Yes." Janet nodded. And then to me, "His accent is so sexy."

Mary seized the opportunity to poke the bear. "What? Patty, you didn't know?"

Patty's hand gripped into a fist. "That butler didn't tell me. I'm going to give him a piece of my mind." She stormed out, her sensible shoes slapping against the floor.

"Ha! He didn't tell her? That's my boy." Cook grinned cheekily.

"I guess he doesn't like her either," Mary added.

"I'd say not. He overheard something she said to Marguerite, and apparently it was not nice."

"What do I do?" Janet asked. "The table wasn't set for two."

Cook shrugged. "Not our worry. It's Patty's problem. Remember, she's the head housekeeper." Still, she assembled another plate.

A moment later, Patty rushed back in. Cook held out the plate, and Patty snatched it from her, her cheeks flushed.

I finished the salad and dished it onto two frosty plates from the freezer. My fingers felt like ice as I carried them out to the dining room. Mary followed with the dressing decanters.

I couldn't wait to finally meet the elusive guest known as "Miss Janice's special friend." And, amazingly, he lived up to my every expectation. His slicked-back hair and a goatee were lightly speckled with gray. His clothing showed impeccable taste, and he even had a red silk handkerchief in his well-tailored dinner jacket pocket.

I could have stared all I wanted because the two of them were completely engrossed in their private conversation, broken only by soft laughter. Miss Janice appeared to have recovered from her earlier skeleton fright.

Gerald leaned back in his chair as I approached.

"Thank you, my dear," he murmured as I set the plate down. Janet was right. His accent was sexy.

Through the next couple of hours, we brought out four different courses. Miss Janice and Gerald took their dessert into another room, and we were free to clear the table. Apparently, after her bedroom turn-down, Miss Janice did not require a sleep tonic, so we were excused for the evening.

The last we saw of Patty was of her rounded, exhausted shoulders as she slunk toward the guest bedroom while we finished cleaning the kitchen.

At nine o'clock, I headed to my room. It had been a long day, and my legs felt weak and weary. On the stairs, my ankle gave a little zing to remind me of how I'd turned it in my search for Hank. At the landing, I paused to pat the giant chess knight statue for good luck. I could hear Gerald and his great booming voice with Miss Janice in the cigar room.

Once in my room, I grabbed my drawing pad and flopped onto the bed. Hank already waited for me on my pillow. I rubbed his neck and then started sketching Gerald, turning the drawing into a cartoon caricature. I gave the man a teacup and drew his pinky poking out.

My gaze landed on the leather envelope I'd found in the house tunnel. In the craziness of the day, I'd forgotten all about it. I leaned to pluck it off the dresser. A string held the envelope closed. Carefully, I unwound it.

Dirt crumbled off and fell to the floor. It turned out to contain a letter. Excited, I smoothed it out to read. Hank came over to sniff it.

"What did you find for me?" I asked the cat and scratched his ears.

Dear Nelson,

I'm finally home and find everyone gone from the house. It's strange and I really would love to talk with you. Like our old days with kings and queens and treasures and pomme de terre.

Of course life must go on, and with Madeline Escott as the guide, we'll find our way. Three steps forward and two sideways. Silence met or to the ground with me it will go.

Hopefully you will be back soon. I'm tired of adventure yet there still seems to be one left. I left you a little something in the library. Tell no one.

Sincerely yours-

The post script was smeared. A small drawing had been sketched at the bottom, little dashes with an x in the center. I counted the dashes, but they didn't seem to correlate with either three or two. Why was this left in the tunnel? It read a little strange but seemed harmless. Why hide it there?

Just then, there was a knock on my door.

CHAPTER FIVE

*M*ary stood there, bearing a napkin full of cookies—my favorite kind of guest. "Ten o'clock. Ready for book club?"

"Yeah, but first come and check out what I found."

She placed the cookies on the dresser and carefully took the letter from me. "What the heck? A treasure map?" Her eyes narrowed. "Did you get this from a cereal box?"

I groaned at her heartless reaction to my excitement. "Ha, ha, ha. This is what Hank was sitting on in the tunnel. What do you think?"

She shrugged and grabbed a cookie. "I'd be more excited about it if the treasure wasn't a potato."

"What are you talking about?" I leaned over the paper.

"Didn't you read this? See for yourself." She pointed to the bottom.

"It says pomme de terre."

"Yea. A potato. Like I said."

Well, that was disappointing. Who wanted to look for a bunch of potatoes? "It's probably not linked to Bernie then."

"You think he's the one who left it?"

I nodded. "Why would it be in the tunnel if it wasn't important?"

She lifted a shoulder. "Who knows with this crazy house. I'm already overwhelmed. There was a freaking skeleton in the house! Just don't make me go back in the wall again. I swear I can still feel spiders crawling on me. They watch you with all eight eyes, you know." She shoved the rest of the cookie in her mouth and google-eyed at me.

I snorted. "Eight eyes, huh?"

"At least! Maybe more. They're serious about keeping an eye on you. Today reminded me of being stuck in a hospital elevator when I was visiting one of my cousins after his appendicitis surgery." She shivered. "The elevator door closed, and then the stupid thing clunked. It wouldn't move at all. I pushed every button, but nothing happened. Even worse, no one came to help for what felt like forever…."

"That sounds horrible!"

She nodded. "So I'm rather proud of myself for going in the house at all. And facing spiders. I feel like a rock star." She did a superstar move.

This time I laughed. "Listen, you never have to go in there again. Maybe Cook knows the answer to this letter. She's been here forever." I packed up the folder to bring with me and scratched Hank's head goodbye.

"I'll tell you one thing, Mr. Gerald is a godsend," Mary said emphatically.

"Yeah?"

"Haven't you noticed how calm and happy he makes her? I can only imagine the meltdown she'd be having over Mr. Bones without him. She hasn't even said a peep about what the cops did to her flower bed."

"How did she meet him?"

"At the butcher shop, if you can believe that."

"What? No way." As far as I knew, Miss Janice never left the house except for charity functions and dinner parties.

"She wasn't by herself. She'd gone with the neighbor, Mrs. Fitzwater, to some holiday gala. The story Cook told me was that they passed Gerald Hawkings's limo broken down on the road. Mrs. Fitzwater recognized him, so they stopped."

We tip-toed out into the hallway, and I shut the bedroom door. As we sidled down the hallway, I felt like a kid

44

sneaking out of bed to spy on the parents' dinner party. I wasn't as afraid of being caught by Miss Janice. It was Patty. If she saw us, who knew what she'd do.

Mary opened Marguerite's bedroom door, and we quietly entered. The room appeared sad and limp without the lively presence of our head housekeeper. She walked over to the bookshelf and reached for the third shelf. The board clicked as she pressed it, and the entire shelf swung open. Flickering candlelight and cheery voices ushered us into the hidden room.

"Hi, loves," Cook chirped from her armchair. She cheerfully wiggled her toes from the footrest. "Snacks over there." She pointed to a table decked out with a tea set and pastry platter.

Mary snuggled into the chair next to her, and Cook passed her a cookie from her plate. I found my favorite ottoman and curled up on it, tucking my feet under me. Movement from below the corner of the makeshift bookshelves caught my attention. Hank poked his head out from the bottom board and sauntered out into the room. He saw me looking and meowed, but Lucy held out a bit of cookie to entice him. He paused to give it a sniff, and she picked up his heavy beanbag body and settled him on her lap. Then she rubbed his ears to convince him to stay.

"I just love cats," she said. "I miss my little Samson back home."

"So, who wants to discuss the little wooblie we found in the wall today?" Cook asked, brushing crumbs off her generous chest.

"Wooblie?" Janet parroted. "That's definitely not the word I'm thinking of. I want to know how long he's been there?"

"Long enough to become a bag of bones." Mary grinned.

"That's not humorous," Jessie said with a tip of her chin.

"To think we walked up and down those back steps with him sitting right on the other side." Lucy shivered.

I rubbed my arms at the disturbing thought. "You know for sure it was Bernie?"

"Bernie Riley Thornberry. He never was without that watch you found. If I recall, his grandfather actually had it made for him for his graduation present years ago." She clucked her tongue. "The poor man. We thought he'd disappeared in the Amazon on an expedition. Those wretched years of not knowing, and here he was all along in the house."

"How could no one notice him? I mean...." Mary let the thought hang, but the nuance was obvious.

"The summer he disappeared, TB was running rampant in the city. Everyone left for the country to escape."

"Isn't this the country?" I asked, confused.

"True, it is. But with the servants gone, it was too much for old Ms. Thornberry. She was eighty at the time. Her sister took her in, along with the rest of us staff."

All the Thornberry names were confusing me. "Who was she?"

"Mr. Thornberry and Bernie's mom." She shook her head, examining the watch once again. "Bernie was just back from overseas. He'd gone to Ireland straight after high school. Left with his friend who was writing a book—his masterpiece, his friend called it. Privately, Bernie once told me it was a stinking pile. Bernie was hired to take pictures for it."

"He was a photographer?" Mary asked.

"He was and a darn good one, I heard tell, despite his own insecurities."

"What's the name of the book?"

"We heard it was lost for good in some mysterious accident. Bernie came back home and stayed at the estate. It was actually an unpleasant surprise for us when we all returned to the manor. The place was a wreck. It took us forever to get the living room back to sorts. My goodness, I don't even want to tell you where I found the throw pillows! Bernie had been doing a bit of partying with his friends, I imagine."

"But he wasn't here when you returned?"

"Nope. The last we heard was a call that he was off to tour the Amazon. As time passed with no word from him, everyone feared the worst."

"How horrible," Lucy breathed.

Cook nodded and wiggled her toes on the ottoman, her bare feet red and calloused. "Travel wasn't as safe back in those days, and getting information from other countries was sketchy. The family mourned, but eventually, everyone moved on."

"And he was never heard of again?"

"Nope, nor his author friend. We assumed the author friend stayed in Ireland, heartbroken that his manuscript disappeared, along with all of Bernie's photos." She tapped her chin. "Poor Bernie's disappearance devastated Old Ms. Thornberry. She died soon after, some say of a broken heart."

"And here he was all this time in the house. Terrible." Mary shook her head.

Cook nodded. "Come to think of it, it was maybe a year or so later that Mr. Thornberry began courting Miss Janice. And life went on."

I figured this was a good time to bring out the leather envelope. "I found this in the tunnel today. Maybe you can make some sense of it."

"What is this, now?" Cook took the package for me and gave it a slight shake. The slim piece of paper slipped out. "Is this a letter?"

"Yes, I just wish the postscript wasn't smudged out."

The other girls leaned in to see it as Cook pulled on her glasses and held it under the oil lamp to read. She squinted. "Well, it's not really something I'd think Bernie would have said. But it sure looks like his handwriting. They went to that private school that taught writing P's with just that swirl. His literary friend must have rubbed off on him." She passed it back to me, and I carefully folded it and replaced it in its envelope.

"I wonder what's going to happen with the police investigation," Janet mused.

"The police say it looks like a construction accident. With it happening so long ago, I don't think they're going to investigate it much." Cook shrugged.

I reread the letter. "I wonder who Nelson is?"

Cook reached for another cookie. "Oh, that's easy. He was the old butler way back when."

My mouth dropped. "You knew him?"

"Sure I did. Nelson Morgan was here when I first started. Looks like Bernie was telling him goodbye before he left for the Amazon. Nelson was a good friend to him, maybe even a father figure, in some ways. They used to play chess together in the evenings."

"When did Nelson leave?"

"He retired thirty-odd years ago. That's when we got Butler."

"You've been here longer than Butler?" Janet gasped. I understood. Butler seemed like he was a part of the very foundation of the house.

Cook narrowed her eyes, obviously not pleased at Janet's shock. "I told you, I started here as a young woman, a girl, really. Back then, many of us struck out on our own at that age."

Janet nodded and tried to smooth it over. "You look half his age, so I was surprised."

That compliment worked like butter on warm bread, and Cook smiled as she settled back into her cushion.

"I wish I could have been here back then and met those people," I murmured.

Cook mumbled around her bite. "You still can. I know where he is. Although I'm not sure how much he will remember."

My eyebrows raised. "What do you mean? You know where who is?"

"Nelson Morgan. He's at the Rosewood Nursing Home over in Granite. Though he's probably pushing a hundred now."

My mouth dropped. "You think he'd remember any of this?"

"He's always been as sharp as a tack, but you never know. Time can be such a thief. Still, the only way to find out is to visit the place and meet him yourself."

CHAPTER SIX

There was no time to spare a visit to the nursing home for the next few days. Patty kept us working hard. Cook hated the makeover to her pantry, and dinner was earlier than ever. But what worried me the most was that Patty seemed to have curried favor with Miss Janice. Patty had discovered how to concoct Gerald's favorite drink, and now he praised her up to high heaven. Of course, this pleased Miss Janice. In fact, I'd never seen Miss Janice smile so much. We really needed Marguerite to return from her vacation and fast.

Still, Patty couldn't keep us from taking our weekly afternoon off. When that day arrived, Mary and I made plans together.

I brought afternoon tea out to the sunroom to serve Miss Janice and Gerald. The room really was my favorite place. Lattice panes in the window caused the sun to stripe the floor in light. Miss Janice's shoes were in one such stripe, and I could see by the way she tapped her toes, she liked the sun's warmth.

"I heard you and Mary have plans later," Miss Janice addressed me as I set down the tray. She lifted a cup and waited.

Her question caught me a bit off guard. Normally, she didn't care about our affairs. "Yes, that's right."

"Patty wanted to be sure it was clear with me. Of course, I reminded her everyone gets a break." She took a small sip.

My shoulders relaxed. "We're actually visiting an old employee."

"Oh?"

"Nelson Morgan. He was once the old butler here."

There was a pause, and you could almost see Miss Janice riffling through her mental memory banks. Then she smiled gently. "Nelson. I remember him. He left a few years after Henry and I married. He's still alive?"

"Perhaps you should pay him a visit soon," Gerald suggested, his accent deep and sultry.

Her eyes locked on his. "My dear, he'd hardly remember me after all this time."

"How could anyone forget someone as charming and radiant as yourself?"

She gave him a good-natured swat on his hand, but her pink cheeks showed she was obviously pleased. She turned back to me. "Please give him my regards."

I assured her I would and left the room.

A short time later, Mary and I found ourselves in her battered little car headed that way to deliver the message.

"And away we go!" Mary shouted, racing down the road. Her brakes squealed at the stoplight, and then we tore off again, jerking me in my seat.

"So, what do you think about Bernie Thornberry?" I asked, rather breathlessly.

"I think it's interesting he was a photographer. I wonder what happened to the manuscript."

"What do you think of the letter?"

Mary stepped on the gas harder. "It makes me wonder why he wrote to Nelson instead of his dad."

"Cook said he thought of the butler as a father figure."

"I wonder if Nelson ever got the letter?" She lit into the curve in the road in such a way that my eyebrows flew up.

I checked my seatbelt. "If he did, how did it end up deep inside the house?"

"What do you think Bernie was doing under there anyway?"

I shivered.

"What?" Mary asked as she turned into the nursing home parking lot.

"I wonder if he was hiding."

"His letter?" she asked, pulling into a parking stall.

"Or himself."

With that horrible thought, we both walked into the nursing home.

I opened the door, and we stepped into the reception area. We were immediately accosted by the scent of chicken soup and a weirdly flashing strobe light. A fluorescent bulb overhead was responsible for the light, flickering as though being beaten by a captured moth.

A small ladder stood in the center of the reception area with a young man in beat-up tennis shoes balancing at the top. He grunted as he tried to pry off the plastic cover. Staring up from the bottom was a woman wearing blue scrubs, thick-soled shoes, and a long yellow cardigan.

She crossed her arms impatiently. "Scout, you doing okay?"

"Almost got it." Of course, at that moment, the plastic cover clattered to the ground. The woman ducked, yelling.

"I warned you not to stand there, didn't I?" he defensively hollered back.

She wasn't having any of his sass. "I'm about to tell you what, that's what."

"Sorry, sorry." He grimaced as he plucked the bulb from the socket and then gently swapped it with the one resting on the top of the ladder.

"You just give that to me before it falls as well," demanded the nurse.

He passed it down to the woman and screwed in the other. When he had finished, she lifted up the plastic cover to him. Steady light streamed into the room, and she smiled with satisfaction. Then she turned to us. "Can I help you?"

I smiled. "We're here looking for one of your residents. Nelson Morgan."

"I see." Although clean of makeup, her pale eyelashes didn't detract from her surprised look. "Nelson Morgan? You're sure?"

Just the way she said it shot a shard of fear through me that we were too late. Cook did mention he was pushing one hundred.

"Yes," I whispered, scared to hear her response.

She tipped her chin and studied us. "Interesting. His room's usually quite quiet. Do you know him?"

My mouth went dry, but Mary answered for us. "He's an old friend." Of course, she added her sweet hometown smile that always instilled a bit of sincerity.

The woman seemed persuaded. "I see. He's in room 330. Go down the hall to the left, take the elevator to the third floor and go past the nurses' desk. I'll ring them up to let them know to expect you."

"Great. Thanks." Mary left for the hallway.

I hesitated. "What do you mean his room is usually quiet?"

"He's had another visitor recently." Her eyes glinted curiously. "Has something happened in the family?"

I shook my head. "No, nothing that I know of." I wanted to ask if it was a family member who'd visited, but then the question might come back and bite me if she further questioned my identity. I was a horrible liar and now didn't have quick-thinking Mary standing here to help me. So, I smiled instead and hurriedly followed after Mary.

Mary must not have listened to the nurse's directions past the first one because I spotted her wandering after the left turn. I reeled her back in with an urgent whisper, and we soon located the elevators.

"You ready for this?" Mary asked as she jabbed the floor button.

"Yes. I'm excited for some answers."

"Can you just see Cook's face if we come back, knowing how to find Bernie's missing photographs?" She grinned.

The elevator dinged, and after an unusually long pause and a clunk, the doors slid open. Mary tightly gripped my arm. But I only had a second to process her fear of elevators when I saw a muscular young man dressed in a blue Oxford shirt and with a spanking new haircut standing inside. He focused on his phone, typing away. Gradually his gaze slid up distractedly to land on me.

He froze.

I froze.

We were like two ice statues at a doomed wedding.

"Uh, hi," he said and nervously tucked his phone into his pocket.

My shock caused my tongue to feel like a carpet roll. "Hello," I managed to awkwardly croak.

He stepped out of the elevator as his eyes took in Mary and then bounced back to me. He cleared his throat. "So, you're here now?"

"Yeah. I got a job out in the country a while ago. What about you? I'm surprised to see you here." I squeezed my clammy hands tighter.

"Oh, came out this way after school. Really hated living in the city, and the pay this place offered was good. I'm the respiratory therapist."

My eyelids sprang wide before I could control them. "Wow."

He nodded and rocked uncomfortably on his feet. "It's a good job. This is my Tuesday route."

Then his phone buzzed, and I think we all stared at it in relief. He pulled it out and gave it a quick glance. "Well, maybe I'll see you around. I'm sure we'll run into each other again soon."

"Sure. Another time then. See you later," I said lamely.

He waved and turned away. I waved too, but he didn't see, hurrying as he was down the hallway, which made my wave even more awkward. I cringed and turned to board the elevator, only to find the doors shut. Mary jabbed the button again, and the doors immediately opened.

"What was that all about?" Mary hissed, looping her arm through mine and dragging me onboard.

"Just someone I once knew," I murmured. I really wasn't ready to go into it at the moment. Especially with still reeling at having him land like a booby trap out of nowhere.

"Really. Sounds like a good story." Her eyes glinted, and the corner of her lip tipped up.

I shook my head. "Nah. Boring like everything else."

"Well, by the look in his eye, I strongly bet you're wrong. By the way, you looked more ruffled than I'd ever seen you before."

"It's no big deal. Okay, let's get back to the game plan."

She wouldn't relent. "He really shook you. Does he at least have a name?"

My cheeks heated like two stove burners. "Chris."

The elevator chimed, and the doors opened. The nurses' station was empty, so there was no need to check-in. I led the way down the hall and read the numbers of the rooms. Finally, we came to room 330. Blue curtains over the window blocked the view of the room.

"Ready?" I asked. Mary nodded. Lifting my chin, I knocked on the steel gray door.

There was no answer.

"Maybe he can't hear you?" Mary tapped her ear to indicate hearing loss. I knocked harder, this time stinging my knuckles against the metal.

No response.

Mary bobbed her head toward the room. "Let's go."

"You mean just walk in?" I glanced around, but the hallway remained empty.

She nodded and confidently turned the handle. We were immediately confronted by a sheeted wall.

"Hello?" I called and gently pushed back the sheet. Its hangers rattled along the metal pole.

An elderly man lay in his bed with the TV softly burbling from the wall. Blankets were pulled up to his chest and tucked under his armpits. His eyes were closed and his mouth open. Dentures floated in a glass on the table next to him.

"He's asleep," I whispered. Mary shoved me forward so that she could shut the door.

"Come on. We're going to wake him." Her mouth settled into a determined line as she walked over to the bed. "Sir? Mr. Morgan? How are you today?" Gently, she shook his arm.

The man wobbled and fell to his side like a piece of fire wood rolling down a hill. People shouldn't move like that. I gasped while Mary covered her mouth.

"He's not asleep," she finally acknowledged.

I thought to prop him back up in case we were wrong. I didn't want his breathing constricted. When I touched him, he felt stiff and cold.

Flinching away, I stared at Mary. Her hand clapped over her mouth in shock. It was then that I looked around the room. There weren't many personal objects of his that I could see. And then I saw it on the floor, nearly hidden by the gurney.

A piece of paper.

CHAPTER SEVEN

*B*efore I had time to process these extraordinary circumstances—let alone pick up the paper—the door clanked opened, and the curtain swooped away like a batwing. A nurse smiled when she saw us. "Oh, I'm sorry. I didn't realize Nelson had visitors." She slipped out the door before we had a chance to respond, nearly shutting it on her white nurse heels.

Mary glanced at the bed and then at me with her eyes as wide as sparrow eggs. "Am I seeing what I think I am?"

I turned the paper over with my shoe. "Yep."

"Natural causes?"

"I don't think he put the IV tube around his own neck, so I'd say no."

She reached for her throat. "Oh, my—"

"You see anything else? We have to be quick before we call for help. Also, be careful where you put your fingerprints."

Mary stared at her fingers, still in shock, and then dug out a pen from her purse. She walked over to the patient's closet. Using the pen, she popped the door open to peer inside. A gray sweater hung on a hanger, and a pair of flattened slippers that looked older than poor Nelson Morgan rested on the closet floor.

With the corner of my shirt, I pulled open a drawer nearest the bed. Books and letters stacked inside so tightly I could barely get the drawer open. I didn't have time to read them, so I quickly peeled one out of the envelope and snapped pictures of it.

"The nurse is coming back!" Mary hissed as she shut the closet door.

I refolded the fragile letter and pushed it back into the envelopes before shoving the drawer shut with my hip.

The same nurse reopened the door, this time her face not so welcoming. "I'm sorry, who are you, again? We don't have any record of you checking in at the nurses' desk."

"No one was there, so we came in. We just tried to wake him up. Something is wrong with Nelson!" Mary unexpectedly shrieked. "He needs help!"

The startled nurse took one look at Mary, one at me, where I clamped my hand over my mouth in my best portrayal of shock, and then ended on the poor butler. Flustered, she ran over, her hands reaching out to take his pulse. She froze when she spotted the IV tube. Undaunted, she checked the pulse and then ran back to the hallway, calling for a code blue.

I waved at Mary, and we followed after the nurse. The nurses' desk was a beehive of activity now.

"You want to leave?" Mary hissed. I shook my head. She tried again. "We should go. They don't know who we are. They might blame us."

"We'll never find out what happened if we leave. Besides, with all the security cameras, we'll end up on prime-time news if we disappear now."

She accepted that bit of information with a very sad frown. There wasn't much to say after that. We came across a set of chairs and tried to stay out of everyone's way.

My hope was that the rushing people would forget about us. I actually thought it worked for a minute because I overheard one nurse ask another for Nelson Morgan's son's phone number.

The second nurse said, "I tried it only a minute ago. He's not answering again."

The first snorted. "Typical. I guess I need to order some steak then."

I blinked at Mary, and she shrugged. What a bizarre comment.

Soon the police were there with their heavy boots and pushing bodies, filling the room and cornering everyone. One officer found us, and we gave a quick statement. Fortunately, the dead man's state of rigor mortis gave us our alibi, so the police let us go on our way.

Sometimes life could feel so surreal, it seemed ordinary. I felt that way now as we walked to the elevator and Mary punched the down button.

"Who would kill a man nearly one hundred years old?" she asked, bewildered.

I shook my head, as confused as she was and checked the piece of paper I'd picked up. Disappointingly, I saw it was simply a receipt for a soda at the hospital cafeteria, and crumpled it.

My stomach tightened as we waited for the elevator to open. Chris better not be there again. This day was one for the books, that was for sure.

Downstairs, the receptionist gave us a curious stare as we walked past her desk. She didn't have time to say anything, what with the phone ringing off the hook even as she held the receiver to her ear. Honestly, I thought she might stop us with a question—her raised eyebrows indicated deep suspicion—but then we were through the front door and outside and finally into freedom. Mary glanced at me, and I thought she felt the same way because her steps sped up, and the next thing I knew she was jogging to the car.

I ran after her. Truth be told, I may have beat her to the little car. Studying the pictures of the letter was next on my list. She unlocked the doors—over a car no one would ever steal with its ancient eight track player and no AC— and we plopped into the front seats like we were playing the nefarious roles of Bonny and Clyde.

Silence dominated for about two beats before we both broke out simultaneously into sentences that jumped over one another.

"Can you believe that just happened?"

"Who would want to hurt a man that old?"

Mary jiggled her keys from her purse and jabbed them into the ignition. She adjusted the mirror and shook out her curls. "Unbelievable."

"And what did the nurse mean about buying a steak?"

"I think I know," Mary said, strapping her seatbelt. I did the same.

"Are you going to tell me?" I asked.

"Sometimes Cook sends me out for pickup at a different butcher shop if she needs something specialized. And guess what it's called."

I raised an eyebrow, waiting for the answer.

"Morgan's Firehouse."

"You're kidding. You think that's Nelson's son?"

"Let's go find out."

"Hold on there. What are we going to do? Rush in with some very bad news? I think we should at least wait until the police meet with him first."

"Come on, let's just go scope it out. Maybe it'll be one of those situations of being at the right place at the right time."

"Yeah, because that worked so well for us in the past." My eyelids shuttered closed. Not excluding what had just happened, we had a whole list of experiences that were all equally as frightful.

Still, it was the best lead we had. I opened up the phone's photos to see if I could read the pictures I'd taken while she swung out onto the road. Between the corners and her stomps on the gas, my stomach rebelled with instant carsickness. I had to give up trying to read them.

We headed back into the main part of town. Soon the scent of fried chicken and onions courted us through the window as we passed a row of chain restaurants. Not too long after, we pulled into the parking lot of a low white building with a different kind of scent. Smokey, and also feral.

Morgan's Firehouse butcher shop.

CHAPTER EIGHT

ary pulled into a space between an old jeep and a pick-up truck. "This is it. You ready?"

I nodded, as ready as I'd ever be, and we stepped out of the car and into smoke-scented air.

"All right, let's go get some answers." Mary's lips settled into a line of determination. She yanked her purse high on her shoulder and strode into the butcher shop.

It was surprisingly crowded inside the tiny room. Two customers left when we entered, and a man and woman waited at the counter. A young woman behind the cash register filled a cardboard box with white paper-wrapped packages.

It didn't look like a place where we could hide unseen.

"What's the plan?" I whispered.

The man gathered his box in his arms, all the while talking about the nice-sized rib steaks included inside. His wife held the door open, and they argued about how to prepare them as they left.

We still did not have a plan.

As always, Mary never appeared worried. She sauntered confidently up to the counter and smiled at the woman on the other side. "Hey, how are you doing today? How are the kids?"

My eyebrows practically flew off my forehead. The gal on the other side seemed equally taken back, but she covered with a professional smile. "They're good. How are you?" It was obvious she had no idea who Mary was, but she was adept at faking.

"Oh, I'm fine, other than my kid's soccer coach constantly rescheduling practice." Mary leaned against the butcher block with a weary sigh. I swiftly stared up at the dry-erase board that advertised their prices to avoid choking.

The cashier relaxed with a chuckle and straightened the display of steak sauces. "Isn't that the truth? And when they finally do, it's always smack dab at dinner time."

"Right?" Mary grinned.

"Now, what can I get you?"

"Well, I was going after a chuck roast, but after hearing your last customer, I think I'd like two of your rib steaks, if that isn't too much trouble."

"Not at all. We have some nice ones back here." The woman disappeared through clear plastic doors.

"That was quick thinking about her kids. How did you know?" I asked.

She nodded her head toward the painted cinder block wall behind the counter. Squinting, I spotted a picture taped to the wall, two kids with big grins, both clad in soccer uniforms.

"Brilliant," I muttered as the woman came back through the swinging doors.

"What do you think?" the woman said, holding up the thick packages. "These are an inch and a quarter thick."

"Perfect!" Mary beamed. "And how about this sauce? I remember when the butcher recommended it to me."

The gal grabbed the bottle and added it shook her head. "Aww, Terry. He didn't come in today. Poor guy got some really bad news. His father died."

"Oh, no! I'm so sorry," Mary gasped while I made likewise sympathetic noises. But how did Terry find out his dad died so fast?

The door opened, and Mrs. Fitzwater's chauffeur walked in. He ignored us, his eyes locked on the menu board — obviously a man on a mission.

"Hello," I said while Mary paid for the meat.

His eyes lit with recognition. "Oh, hi there, Laura Lee. What are you doing here?"

"Getting dinner for Miss Janice. You?"

By now, Mary had her purchases tucked under her arm.

"Same," he said. "Mrs. Fitzwater is outside waiting in the car. She's had a craving for steak."

"Well, this place is amazing," Mary said and nudged me toward the door. I glanced at my watch and realized we needed to return back to the house. Patty was probably pacing outside to make sure we weren't late. We waved goodbye and hurried out.

Sure enough, Mrs. Fitzwater's black town car was parked two spaces away. I glanced at it curiously. The window rolled down, and an arm waved out, bracelets glittering in the sunlight. "Yoohooo!"

"I'll be right back," I told Mary.

I caught a glimpse of Mrs. Fitzwater's flushed, excited face as I walked over. She must know about the skeleton we'd found in the wall. I knew how much she loved gossip.

"Laura Lee, I'm so glad to see you! I heard! I heard! What's going on over there at Thornberry Manor? I've tried to phone Janice, but she's not taking calls at the moment. A very busy lady, I'm told. Tell me everything!"

She'd fired her comments off fast without a breath taken, and now looked a little pop-eyed as she gasped.

"Hi, Mrs. Fitzwater." I smiled.

"Hop in." She opened the door. "You're returning to the manor? Let my chauffeur take you back."

I glanced at Mary. I couldn't let her face Patty alone. But maybe I could get a little information before I left.

"Unfortunately, I need to go with Mary. Our new housekeeper...."

"Oh, I heard. She's a bear. Now tell the truth. Did they really find Bernie Thornberry?"

I nodded.

She sucked in her breath. "After all these years. I can hardly believe it. I remember when he went missing. I was just an itty bitty girl, but I recall how horribly sad it was."

Since she was around Cook's age, I wasn't so sure how little she'd been, but I made a sympathetic sound.

"I always suspected his friend. He was so jealous of him."

"Jealous?"

"Very. I don't mind telling you they both tried courting me. But then the plague came, and we all separated for the summer."

"Did Bernie have a lot of friends?" I asked.

"He had a couple. Unfortunately, his little group was doomed to stay friends outside of childhood. Terry Morgan was one of them."

"This Terry Morgan?" I jerked my thumb toward the shop.

She fluffed her hair from her eyes with a long, manicured fingernail. "The very same. Of course, he wasn't as hobnob as the other two. He worked at the dairy after high school. Plus, of course, his dad worked for the Thornberry's. As the friends grew older, that mattered in their social class. That might have caused their falling out."

"Falling out," I clarified. "So they didn't remain friends?"

"Sadly no. Soon after school was over, everyone went their separate ways. Seems to be the way of the world."

"And now Terry's a butcher."

"Still not respectable enough. But it's too late for all of them. Too late." She clucked her tongue and shook her head.

Her chauffeur returned, and I said goodbye, puzzling over my new information. Too late, and with a grimace, I realized I hadn't asked about the other friend.

CHAPTER NINE

*N*ot surprisingly, Mary kept the car at a lively pace on the way home, and we arrived with time to spare. We pulled through the Thornberry gate, and a branch fell in front of the car. Stephen stood on a ladder pruning the branches that had broken in the last windstorm. His little sister, Sophia, wove through the rose bushes, her braids flying behind her, her arms out like she was an airplane. The little girl spun in a circle and fell to the sunny carpet of grass.

Mary swerved to the side, and Stephen waved as we drove by. He was already halfway to us by the time Mary parked behind the garage.

"Hey, ladies, how'd it go?" He grinned.

"You mean the steak?" Mary lifted the packages.

He lifted an eyebrow. "I heard you were going to the nursing home."

"Who told you that?" Mary's tone became instantly suspicious.

"Cook, this morning." Stephen wiped the sweat off his forehead with a beefy forearm. "Judging by your faces, you still have no answers, huh?"

I took over. "We went to the home. You're not going to believe it, but we were too late."

"What? He'd already passed?" Stephen shot me an incredulous gaze.

I nodded. "And we're pretty sure he was murdered."

Stephen's face went through an interesting transformation as a slide show of emotions slid across it. Finally, he settled down into a mostly neutral expression. "Why? Who would have done it?"

"No idea. It doesn't make sense. However, we did track down Nelson's son. Three guesses on who he is." Mary gestured to the steak again.

"Terry Morgan, the butcher? Oh, yeah, I already knew that. How's he taking it? Poor guy."

My mouth dropped open. Stephen already knew what had taken us all afternoon to find out. "He didn't go to work today, so I guess he's pretty upset. And understandably so. How do you know him?"

"My dad went to school with him when his dad was the butler here. He had some stories."

"Oh, interesting. Did your dad like Terry?" It occurred to me then just how weird it was that Stephen had lived at the Thornberry Manor nearly all of his life and that his Dad had worked here, too.

"Actually, I think Terry was the guy who sort of sparked Mr. Thornberry's paranoia of his stuff being stolen. That's when Mr. Thornberry started designing all these secret rooms and stuff."

I'd wondered what had made Mr. Thornberry steer in that direction. Most people don't own a house thinking about how to create secret tunnels and gardens. "So those passageways weren't always here?"

"Some maybe, but Mr. Thornberry definitely expanded them."

"What happened?"

"It was Halloween ages ago. The old butler Nelson was here still."

I cringed when Stephen said that, thinking of the man we'd found in bed.

CATASTROPHE IN THE LIBRARY

"Well, that evening, someone broke into the window in the back door. It was a mess. Glass everywhere. Poor Cook stepped on some and cut her foot."

My interest pricked. I needed to ask her about that.

"Nelson got together with Mr. Thornberry and said he knew someone who could come out immediately to fix the window. Mr. Thornberry let Nelson handle it all. Late that night, a handyman came and fixed the door."

"That doesn't sound too suspicious," I said.

"All was going well until the handyman was discovered in the library."

"What?" I gasped. "What was he doing in there?"

Stephen shrugged and plucked a stray leaf from the bush. "No one knows."

"He must have had a reason."

"He said he was looking for the bathroom. The thing is, Mr. Thornberry had some very valuable things from his travels. He freaked out. It was then that dad told me he started hiding things. And even worse, one of the trinkets Bernie had brought home disappeared."

"So the handyman took it?"

"I don't see how he could. Nelson escorted him from the house, and he certainly would have seen it if the handyman

79

had been carrying it. And Nelson was a big man. Gentle with kids but a real bear to any threats."

The man I'd seen had been thin, but his hands had been huge. From what Cook said, Nelson had been close to Bernie. I could see the old butler gently patting the head of Bernie as a little boy before sending him to the kitchen to get some cookies.

"What was it?" I asked.

"My dad didn't tell me. Just that it was gone."

"And they never found it again?"

He shook his head. "Never."

"Did they ever find out who broke the back door?"

"Nope, not that either."

"Laura Lee," Mary hissed. "I think I saw Patty staring out the window. We have to go!"

"Bye, Stephen!" I waved and jogged after Mary around the house to the back door. As I entered, I pictured the door all those years ago with the window broken out. It wasn't hard to imagine, especially with the recent destruction of the wall temporarily boarded with some old pallets.

We snuck inside, and I quietly shut the door behind us. The kitchen bustled with life, and the air was saturated with the wonderful scents of roasted meat, sautéed onions, and spicy apples. At the counter, Janet worked on a salad while Jessie peeled potatoes. Margie whipped gravy, and Cook bustled about carving a gorgeous turkey.

"Wow! What's the occasion?" I asked while Mary slipped the steaks into the freezer.

"Gerald Hawkings is here. He's said he's never had a traditional turkey dinner, so Miss Janice has had us working all day to be sure to impress him." Cook spun to get the platter, and her skirt twisted with her.

I desperately wanted to ask her some questions about what Stephen had told me, but I spied Patty in the corner. She stared at me with arms crossed over her chest and the lines writing disapproval around her mouth. "Should you be standing here?"

"I'm sorry?"

"Aren't you supposed to be upstairs and dressed for service?"

"Oh, yes! Sorry." It wasn't actually time yet. Usually, Cook had me arranging flowers and gathering plates. But I wasn't about to argue with Patty.

I ran to the stairs with the intention of patting the knight statue for good luck. If I ever needed good luck, it was now while facing dinner service under Patty's critical eye and Miss Janice's new boyfriend's attention.

Wait, was the library door cracked open? I paused, confused. The door *was* cracked, just a sliver of a dark line to show the doors weren't flush.

Miss Janice had forbidden anyone from entering that room. I walked down the hallway and stood outside the room. Then I heard a strange noise that reminded me of a snake. Hissing. Not waiting any longer, I grabbed the lion door handle and wrenched the door open.

A man whirled around from the fireplace.

CHAPTER TEN

The man saw me and choked. I recognized him right away, Miss Janice's boyfriend, Gerald Hawkings.

"What are you doing in here?" I asked. It was then I noticed Hank crouched a few feet away. Hank with ruffled fur and wild green eyes. Hank who was intensely angry.

"I heard the cat meowing and thought he might be in trouble," Gerald recovered and answered in his crisp accent.

My eyes narrowed. The man smiled in a smooth way that probably made other women swoon but now made my skin crawl. Hank never acted aggressively to anyone, not even to the dog he loved to bait. Something was up.

"He appears to be alright now," Gerald said, brushing his hands together. It was then I noticed a smear of soot on one hand and blood on his cuff.

"He seems upset to me." I resisted the urge to put my hands on my hips.

"Yes, well, perhaps he wasn't happy about being locked in this room." Gerald smiled again, and this time his eyebrow flicked up as if trying to include me in on a joke.

I stepped away from the door. Hank hadn't been trapped. He could get away whenever he liked. "So you'll be leaving now?"

"Of course." He bobbed his head and made a move as if to brush back that slicked hair before noticing the ash on his hand. As he walked by, I noticed his gaze flicked toward the wall of empty bookshelves. He smiled again and exited, leaving behind a cloud of wood-scented cologne.

Why had he really been in here? The library was void of furniture and long emptied of any books. I wouldn't have noticed if anything was missing.

I walked over to Hank and scratched his head. The animal hadn't relaxed yet and stared moodily at the door.

"It's okay, buddy. He's gone now." I stroked the cat's stiff back and willed him to loosen up. Finally, Hank seemed to be satisfied that all was clear and gave my hand a little sniff.

His whiskers tickled my palm for a moment, and then he turned to disappear through the crack in the cupboard.

Near the fireplace, the stale air had an odd dusty scent to it. I frowned and glanced about again. Not seeing any signs of disturbance, I walked back to the doors, grabbed the handles, shut them firmly behind me, and headed up to my room to change.

The kitchen was a whirlwind by the time I returned with Patty squawking orders like a demanding parrot.

Mary rushed by, tying her apron. Her eyebrows lifted when she saw me, and I perceived both disdain and frustration in them.

"Hurry! Hurry! Not another minute!" Patty clapped.

Cook actually had sweat cropping up on her forehead as she spun around with a bowl of mashed potatoes. "It's ready," she said, rather glumly.

I missed peppy Cook so much with her sassy comebacks. Patty had sucked the fun out of this job like an emotional vampire.

"Where's your service apron?" Patty snapped at me. I ran to the back and grabbed it. I'd barely tied it on when a bowl of corn casserole was thrust into my hands. Patty carried the centerpiece, the carved turkey.

"Don't think I haven't noticed you were late returning from your little field trip," she hissed as we walked toward the formal dining room. The skin on my neck shriveled.

We walked into the formal dining room, where a lovely table had been laid with silver containers that had been filled with all the feast accoutrements one could hope for. Even though I had the afternoon off, I felt guilty for not being a part of the hard work.

Gerald and Miss Janice sat at one end, with Miss Janice at the head of the table.

I couldn't even look at him. I never felt so awkward in my entire life. How could I ignore the fact that I'd just caught the man in the library?

By his actions, you'd think we'd never met before in our lives, let alone fifteen minutes previous. He sipped his wine and laughed, head tipped back, mouth open wide with confidence. Miss Janice watched him with smiling eyes, her hair in one of those swirly updos that reminded me of a bird's nest. Neither of them paid a lick of attention to me, choosing instead to stare into each other's eyes with hearts and rainbows.

I should've felt a sense of inferiority at this moment. After all, both of these people believed they were head and shoulders above me. But I'd realized success definitely couldn't be judged by appearances. Life was proving to me over and over that people liked to appear happier than they really were.

Speaking of appearances, I did have a problem, though. Namely, how to alert Miss Janice that Gerald might not be all he appeared to be.

I glanced at the doorframe to see Patty staring down at me like an owl zeroing in on a mouse. My body jerked involuntarily, and I covered it by hurrying over to the table with the corn casserole. Task relieved, I dipped my head and hurried back to the kitchen. Still as stressed as ever, Cook dished dessert into tiny crystal dishes.

I hurried over to the sink and started in on the mountains of dirty dishes. "Stephen told me a story about the back door being broken into years ago."

"Oh, yes! I remember. Cut my foot on the glass and bled like a stuck pig. I was a wee young thing back then. Just sixteen. Nelson picked me up like I weighed nothing and carried me to the chair." She finished plating the last dessert and began wiping the counters.

"Stephen mentioned something about the repairman being kind of sketchy."

"Kind of? That was Sly Kenner. We found him in the library snooping through the books. Drunk as a skunk, he was. I thought Nelson would about come unglued. Dragged Kenner out by his ear, he did."

"Did you ever find out who broke the door?"

"Rumor had it that it was the milkman's son. A Halloween prank, but we never caught him."

"What happened to the repair guy?"

"Sly disappeared from town. Moved on, I heard. We all forgot the whole thing because that's when Ms. Thornberry really began to believe something had happened to poor Bernie on his travels. She never was the same after that. Poor thing."

I was about to tell her how I'd found Gerald skulking about in the library when we heard a loud clearing of the throat and turned to see Patty's steely glare.

"I assume dessert is ready to be served?"

Cook scowled but walked over and began setting the dishes on a tray. Patty grabbed the tray and whisked it off the counter. Without deeming me worthy of another glance, she announced over her shoulder that she expected to see the kitchen finished by the time she returned or our pay would be docked.

"Who does she think she is?" muttered Cook, who grabbed a cleaning rag. "Threatening to dock our pay."

"She's not really staying, is she?"

Cook lifted a shoulder weakly as she wiped. "Marguerite still isn't ready to return home. Last I talked to her, she brought up retirement."

That word sent chills down my spine. What would we do if she retired? Would we be stuck with Patty? What would that mean for me? Could I continue here at Thornberry if Patty stayed?

Then I thought of my mom and grandma. I couldn't not work when they were relying on me to help out with money. And what about getting back to college? My student loans were like this mountain of dishes, even though I hadn't finished with school yet. Frustrated, I slapped the rag in the soapy water.

"Let's not fret about that right now," she said, patting my arm. "The estate has weathered worse challenges than this. We'll get through even if Marguerite doesn't return."

She didn't look like she believed her own words. But she wasn't the only one who could fake a positive attitude. I'd do what I needed to do, as well.

Together, we scrubbed down the kitchen and had everything sparkling by the time Patty returned. But that still didn't remove the sour expression from her face.

When I left the kitchen, I happened to see Miss Janice and Gerald enter the family living room. Gerald lingered at the doorway. He glanced my way and our eyes locked. His eyes narrowed every so slightly. I swear I detected a threat there, and goosebumps trickled down my spine. Who was this guy, anyway? I needed to find out.

Later that night, when all the chores were finished, I dragged myself upstairs where Hank already waited for me in a scuffled circle of blankets at the foot of the bed.

"What was that all about today?" I asked him. "What was Gerald doing in the library when you found him? And did you scratch him? Is that why he had blood on his cuff?" I stroked his back, and he rubbed his cheek against my hand. "My little guard cat. Here you go." I gave him a piece of sausage I'd purloined earlier as a reward. He sniffed it as though disinterested, so I set it down on the counterpane. After a moment (when he thought I wasn't watching) he carefully took a nibble. I, of course, looked away while he ate.

I reached for my phone and went to social media. What was Gerald's full name? I think I remembered Janet saying Hawkings. I typed it in.

Oddly, nothing popped up about him. Not a thing. Maybe I hadn't typed it in right. I tried different variations of the name. Still nothing. How strange.

I remembered how Cook said the repair guy had disappeared. I wondered if there was anything on him. My thumbs raced across the keyboard to type in Sly Kenner while Hank crunched the last bite.

"Was that good?" He acted like he didn't hear me but washed his face with a rather satisfied air.

Just then, Kenner's name popped up in the search results. I was surprised to see the guy still lived in the area with a home address out in the country a few towns from here.

I rubbed my neck. Would Kenner remember the window repair all those years ago? How could he forget getting nearly beat up? Was he drunk like Cook had said? Or had he faked it after getting caught in the library?

CHAPTER ELEVEN

I still couldn't believe I'd found Kenner. And in the town of Lochsloy, not more than twenty minutes from here. Twenty minutes there, twenty minutes back… I mentally added up the time. He might not have stolen the trinket, but he might have given me some insight as to who would have murdered Nelson. Would a grudge from years ago constitute a motive?

I bit my thumbnail. I wanted to know. I really did. My gut told me he was key somehow. But I knew better than to visit him alone. He had to be up there in years, given how long ago this all was, but that didn't make him less dangerous.

Nervously, I jetted a text off to Stephen. **—Hey, what are you doing tomorrow?**

—Why?

I read it, and the corner of my thumbnail found its way back to my mouth. How could I tell him I wanted someone a little intimidating with me as I waltzed into a strange man's house. I decided to stall. —**Tomorrow at two?** That was my normal lunchtime.

—**Why?** His persistence was annoying.

I had a feeling he wasn't about to go along with my idea willingly. —**Can you drive?**

—**Okay. Where we going?** He'd swapped his why question. Clever.

I sent a smiley face with—**Have to get some sleep. I'll explain tomorrow.**

He sent me a suspicious smiley face back, but I could tell I had him on the hook.

I finished with —**See you out by the garage.**

THE NEXT DAY, I practically danced through my chores as excitement fueled my energy at finding Kenner. I could barely wait to see what the man had to say happened all those years ago. Would he confess? Maybe. After all, he might want to meet his maker with a clean conscience.

Patty kept me busy refreshing all the linens in the bedroom and baths. I cleaned windows and mopped floors. But even she couldn't keep me past my scheduled lunchtime at two o'clock.

As I ran down the stairs to meet Stephen, I patted the statue for good luck with the Kenner meeting. Come on, baby, bring luck now!

Outside, I blinked in the bright sunshine, feeling as free as a kid playing hooky on a spring afternoon. Stephen pulled his car from behind the garage, and I waved at him.

"Hey, you," he said as I climbed into his car. It was a nice-looking vehicle, newer, and judging by the polished dash and clean floor, he really took care of it.

"Hi," I answered, with my phone out and already jabbing in directions. I gave him the route to Kenner's address. He sent me a little side-eye and headed that way.

"You going to tell me where we're going?" he asked as we rolled down the driveway and onto the road.

"Remember the story you were telling me? About the old butler, Nelson, chasing out the repair guy?"

"Yeah?" His eyebrows furrowed. It wasn't an enthusiastic response.

I examined my nails, nervously. "I found him. The repair guy. His name is Sly Kenner."

"You're kidding, right?" Stephen stared out at the trees.

"I'm kind of bad at jokes."

We turned off the main road and down a much narrower track. The trees closed in over the pavement in a threatening way.

I swallowed and gestured in front of us. "Just a little bit farther."

He squeezed the steering wheel. "We're meeting Kenner."

This was going much worse than I expected. I should have just asked Mary to accompany me. "Yep."

"You're not kidding. What are you planning to say?"

My phone announced the destination was coming up, cutting off my response. Which was good, because I didn't have one. Playing it by ear sometimes worked for me, and that's what I was counting on now.

We approached a tiny driveway nearly hidden by thick underbrush overgrown on each side.

I pointed to the driveway. "There. Between all those ferns."

He turned down it and drove slowly, the tires crunching on the gravel. "Kind of scary out here."

The trees shadowed the inside of the car, and I silently agreed. My premonition suddenly screamed to turn around. What had I gotten us into?

"There it is," he said grimly. A tiny house, a shack really, with mismatched roofing and red carpet on the stairs peered out from a gnarled nest of tree branches with suspicious shuttered eyes. Behind it was more of the grove of rotting trees.

Stephen rolled to a stop in the middle of the driveway and glanced up at the moss-covered branches overhead. I winced. He must have been thinking about a branch falling on his car, but there was no safe place to park.

With his jaw clenched, Stephen got out. I followed. We walked up to the door. I realized then that the place was abandoned. No one lived here. After all this, it was a dead end.

Then the barking started, and a white-faced terrier nosed open the screen door.

"Parker! Who's there, boy?" A shadowy figure appeared in the doorway.

"Mr. Kenner? My name's Stephen Markson."

"Don't want anything, and if I owe you, you ain't getting anything. Get off my porch."

"I'm not a bill collector, and I don't want to sell you anything," Stephen said calmly with his palms up.

"Then what are you here for?"

Stephen hesitated, so I jumped in. "Hi, Mr. Kenner. I'm Laura Lee Smith. I've been doing a little research into one of the older families in the area, and I have a few questions for you."

"'Questions? I don't think I can help."

"Maybe not, but I'd like to ask you all the same."

His red-rimmed bleary eyes locked onto mine, and he rubbed his whiskered chin. Parker sat, panting, and Kenner's hand absentmindedly went down to stroke the dog's head while he considered.

"Don't like the look of you," he said to Stephen. His gaze came back to me. "You, I like. You've got five minutes."

He backed away from the door. After a deep breath, Stephen grabbed the rusty handle and opened it despite its protesting squeal.

We walked inside.

My heart sank at the interior. Rough planks, the cracks filled with dirt, made up the floor. A hand-made wooden counter sat under a grimy window, its surface stacked with filthy dishes. Instead of a refrigerator, an ice chest sat underneath, and a cot in the corner. And the scent...the scent was deplorable.

It obviously had no effect on Kenner, despite his large, beet-shaped nose. I looked around for a place to sit. The small table had a single folding chair. The dog went over to a folded blanket on the floor and collapsed with a nasally groan.

Kenner took the chair and stared up at us. "So? What are your questions?" He grabbed for a cigar that looked well abused and held it in a swollen-knuckled hand.

I started. "It's about the Thornberry Estate. Do you remember working there once?"

"Once. Twice. Who's counting?"

"The last time you were there, there was a skirmish between you and the butler?"

He snorted. "That old guy?" He chuckled, his laughter wheezy and low. "I haven't thought of the old guy in years. Yeah. He was suspicious and following me around. I think he used me as a diversion. Wrongly accused me of stuff that he swiped himself."

I frowned. This was an angle I hadn't considered. I didn't want to tell Kenner that Nelson had died. "So, how did you know the butler, Nelson?"

"Nelson? I'd never met him before that day."

I raised my eyebrows. "He recommended you."

"I'm sure someone recommended me to him. Maybe the guy who hired me originally. That's who you should be talking to."

Who else would have hired him from the house? "Was it Mr. Thornberry?"

"No one who lived in the house."

I nodded. Now, this was making more sense. "What were you hired to do then? Not fix the door?"

"I was told to go find something."

That had to be the thing described in the letter. "That's why you were in the library. Did you find it?"

He smirked. "They said the secret is in the library. But I don't remember if I found it or not."

He remembered everything else, but he couldn't remember if he found the treasure? "I see."

I glanced around his small house. It was hard to believe he did find a treasure, what with the squalor he found himself in now. The fireplace smoke mixed with nicotine tar left a sooty residue over everything. His bed was nothing more than a cot covered in messy blankets.

"You need anything?" I asked. I couldn't help it. No one should live like this.

Stephen nudged my foot under the table.

Kenner crossed his arms and studied me. It didn't feel like a sincere stare, instead, his gaze glittered, calculated. "Well, now, you're offering to pay me for some information, finally? I think that's only fair."

I flushed. I had less than ten bucks in my purse, leftover from when I bought stamps. I opened my mouth to answer, but Stephen talked over the top of me. "Listen, I have a twenty. But I don't think she's trying to buy information. I think she feels sorry for you, man."

Kenner didn't like that. "I don't need no dame feeling sorry for me. I get along here just fine. Just the way I want to. Checked out of so-called civilization years ago. All the backstabbing and rat race for the almighty dollar. Get your stuff and get out of here, or I'll throw you out!"

He lunged out of his seat, scaring me. Quickly, I stepped back. Stephen slowly followed, his biceps noticeably tightening under his shirt as his hands clenched.

The two men locked eyes, and Stephen nodded his head. "We'll be leaving then. No one will be throwing us out."

Kenner's threat wasn't viable, not with how the man trembled and tried to steady himself with one gnarled hand against the table. Pity made my stomach turn, an unexpected reaction. I left the room, and Stephen followed after me.

Kenner tried to slam the door behind us. However the poorly-made door barely banged and sounded like it split instead. I tried to look, but Stephen grabbed my shoulder. "Let's get out of here."

CHAPTER TWELVE

*S*tephen drove me back to the manor in less than an hour and a half. It was still within my normal afternoon break, but this job didn't have typical work hours, and Patty could be a terror no matter what.

Mary accosted me as soon as I came through the kitchen door. She seized my elbow and dragged me into the butler's pantry. "I just saw you get out of Stephen's car. Where were you? On a date?"

"What? No!" I protested, surprised. "I tracked down Kenner. You know the repair guy Nelson kicked out of the house? So Stephen came with me to give him a visit."

"Are you serious? Why on earth did you search for Kenner?" Her eyes narrowed in confusion, kind of mirroring how I felt after the visit.

"Long story short, Cook told me this story of how Kenner was hired to repair a broken window, but Nelson caught him in the library. The butler accused Kenner of stealing something, and it was that event that spurred Mr. Thornberry into designing all his crazy hidden rooms to hide stuff."

"What was stolen?"

"Supposedly something Bernie had brought home on his last trip. The rumor is that it was worth a fortune."

"Really? And what was it? Did Kenner take it?"

"If he did steal it, he sure didn't keep any of the money because the man lives in what I'd generously refer to as a shack. It was really heart-rending. As far as what the actual treasure is, that remains a mystery. Kenner didn't say."

"Wow! How intriguing." Her forehead raised thoughtfully. "They say crime doesn't pay. So where do you think Bernie's treasure ended up?"

I shook my head. It seemed like it was another dead end.

"You think that treasure is what Bernie meant when he wrote his letters?"

"Yes. It has to be. How many treasures could one person have left?"

That night in bed, something gnawed at me. Specifically, this one phrase. *Silence met or to the ground with me it will go.* It didn't sound very delighted, like one would be over a treasure. It seemed rather dark.

I searched in my bureau for the letter to read again. There had to be something here. Where had the treasure ended up?

Kenner had insinuated the butler had thrown him out of the house as a distraction—a decoy. I'd only heard great things about Nelson, though.

I typed in the name of Terry Morgan's Firehouse Butcher Shop. I clicked the link, and colored lights flashed with music blaring— all of it screamed success. Butlers couldn't make much money. It made me wonder how his son got the money for this business.

I slipped off my socks and chucked them to the corner. A new theory occurred to me. If Nelson the butler was the one who busted in the library on Kenner, could they have been working together?

That thought didn't sit well with me, especially since everyone appeared to trust Nelson. Even Cook had fond memories of him, and she knew him personally. Could her judgment be that far off?

I knew from experience that sometimes people could surprise you, and not always in a good way.

Pulling on my nightgown, I thought about it some more. What if someone knew Bernie came into some treasure.

Someone attempted to steal it from him, and killed him in the process. Then they came back, broke the window, and tried to snoop some more?

I shook my head. Something wasn't adding up.

I put the envelope away for safety and climbed back into bed. Had Bernie been killed for this letter to Nelson? Had he gone inside the hidden tunnel to hide it? Did someone follow him—a person that Bernie knew?

What about the glass bottle that killed Bernie? Was it a soda bottle? If so, it was not one I'd ever seen before. The bottom was too thick. More like a vase.

The wall cupboard door squeaked open and soft padding came to the end of the bed. Then there was silence. I stared in that direction expectantly, but Hank didn't appear.

"Come on, buddy," I wheedled. He didn't respond. I swear he knew I was anticipating his jump, so he waited until he could catch me off guard to scare me. He'd join me on the bed when he was good and ready and in his own cat time.

"Fine, stay down there then." I leaned back on the pillow. If only I could figure out where he was referring to when he wrote three steps forward and two sideways.

Bernie had two good friends growing up. One was the butcher, and they went their separate ways. They had a falling out, Mrs. Fitzwater had mentioned.

I wondered if I could find more about Bernie, Terry, and the unknown third. I searched for the local high school and was pleased to see that, not only had this school been around for generations, but the school carried yearbooks that dated back that far. I clicked the yearbook link and saw that if I wanted to see a yearbook older than the last ten years, I needed to send in a formal request, and someone would get back to me with the link to the online version.

My heart sang with excitement as I typed the email and then pressed send.

Hank jumped up on the bed. I jerked and squealed before breaking out in laughter. He'd got me again.

He walked over to me, his paws leaving dents in the blankets from his heavy body. Something hung from his mouth like a kitten. I flinched, terrified he'd brought me a prize, one that he'd dug up from inside the walls.

Luckily his present was a pink stuffed toy mouse.

"You love doing that, don't you?"

He bumped his hard head against my hand with his eyes shut and gave me a kitty smile. I chuffed his chin and rubbed his ears, and he thanked me by licking my fingers with his rough tongue. Then he stalked to the end of the bed, where he began kneading the blanket. After a few moments, I heard a deep rumble.

"Aww, you're purring." Purring was a rare occurrence for him, so I appreciated that gift more than his fuzzy toy one.

My phone dinged with a notification. I quickly went to it, amazed that the library had been so quick to respond. Instead, I found a new message—this one from my college email.

I clicked it and read out loud, "You have two weeks before this account is closed. Please check and save your messages before they are deleted." I frowned. "How weird."

Hank lifted his head and britted as in answer. I wiggled my foot to pet Hank, considering the ramifications. I'd had to leave college early to help my mom out several years ago. She was back on her feet, healthy and starting a new life, but I hadn't had the resources or, if I was honest, the motivation to return. It was off my list of things to do for a while.

Because of that, I'd never checked the email account. I'd rarely used it to begin with, and the only messages I'd received had been class updates. Even the teachers had used message boards. I shrugged and started to close it.

Then I hesitated. Closed forever, huh? Maybe I should just check just in case. Did I even remember my old password?

It was the same reason I rechecked locks, alarms, and car doors. I clicked on the link in the message and brought up the account.

It turned out I did remember the password. And there were several new messages, none of which were from the school.

CHAPTER THIRTEEN

$\mathcal{I}$ must have gasped because Hank raised his head and blinked sleepy eyes. The first email was from Chris.

Before I even realized it, I was grinning like a goon. This expression immediately disappeared when I read the date of the message.

Dear *Laura Lee,*

A lot has happened since our breakup. I finished college, and wished you were there when we collected our diplomas. You deserved to be there. I never thanked you for all the help in social science you gave me. I probably wouldn't have passed without you.

Remember our time out at the lake? I'll never forget it. Anyway, I told you about my dad's struggles with alcohol, and how I had to take care of my brothers. I felt like I had no family until my grandfather stepped into the picture.

Things changed when he did. He made me feel like I could accomplish anything. In fact, it was because of him that I tried for a scholarship. Remember when you met him at the restaurant? Man, we had such a good time and laughed so hard.

Anyway, he's sick now. He's not expected to live through the weekend. With mom gone, and dad… busy, I don't have anyone else. My brothers are young and having the time of their lives. They don't understand because they didn't have the same bond with granddad as I did.

Anyway, this is heavy, and I'm not trying to dump on you. Heck, you're probably reading this and telling yourself to run! Just wanted to hear from you. I feel like since you've met him, you'd understand. I know things ended badly between us, but I wish I could hear from you again, if only as friends,

Chris.

My heart hurt to read it. Wow, what had he thought when I hadn't responded? I would have in a second, but he didn't know that. Shame filled my cheeks as I remembered how we ran into each other in the elevator. I wiggled my foot under the blanket as I tried to digest this awkward situation, and Hank watched it with interest.

Should I email Chris back?

I couldn't, not now. I groaned and clicked the light off, staring up into the darkness. Hank pounced and then bit my moving foot through the covers.

"Go to sleep, buddy," I muttered. "At least one of us should."

I BARELY SLEPT and had strange dreams all night. I woke up to a gray morning broken by bird trills. It took me a moment to remember I was not at home with mom making me my first breakfast on summer vacation—but here at the manor. I stretched and blinked the sleep out of my eyes as the scent of bacon I'd been so sure I'd smelled drifted back into dreamworld.

Then the memory of Chris's emails came crashing in on the morning softness. I sat up with a groan. I needed to write something back to him, but the embarrassment was still too intense. Life could pile on confusion at times. I spent so much time lately shaking my head that my neck was in the best shape of my life.

I had to worry about this later. I made the bed and readied myself for the day, including a quick prayer of thanks for all the good things in my life. Starting the day with gratitude almost always changed my outlook, and I needed a change.

Jessie and Cook were already in the kitchen. The sweet aroma of cinnamon rolls danced in the air along with my favorite scent of rich coffee.

I helped myself to a mugful and popped a piece of bread into the toaster for a quick breakfast.

"Good morning, young lady. And how did you sleep?" Cook asked me as she whisked some eggs.

I shrugged. "I had a bad dream about Patty saying she would dock my pay."

Cook rolled her eyes. "Her sense of importance has tripled now that both she and Gerald have made nice."

I found the raspberry jam and butter on the breakfast bar and prepared my toast. Lucy stumbled in, her face puffy from sleep. She picked up a spoon and walked over to the cupboard. I watched her, amused, as she got herself a scoop of peanut butter.

Thinking of Gerald reminded me of how I'd seen him in the library. "How long have they been together? I heard they met outside the butcher shop."

"Odd circumstances but a happy day for this household. You didn't know Miss Janice after her husband died. We didn't even dare to open the curtains for a year straight."

"Mary said Mrs. Fitzwater recognized his limo. How did she know him?" I crunched a bite. Delicious.

"I daresay they met at one of those fancy fundraisers or another. He's not been in the country long. Moved here less than a year ago. Bought that huge manor a mile from here. You know the one with the animal shrubs? He says it reminds him of home." She clucked her tongue. "Used to be one of Bernie's good friend's estate."

"Did Bernie have a lot of friends?"

"A few. Why?"

"I heard a rumor there'd been a falling out with them."

Cook began slicing the vegetables for a spring omelet. "With one, yes. Terry Morgan. During the last years or so, he complained that the Thornberry family was quite unfair to his father. Terry never felt Nelson was paid enough. Now, Bernie tolerated Terry calling him a skinflint, but when he called him an outright thief that ended their friendship. I remember Bernie was quite sad about that. Of course, Nelson never got involved. He was loyal to them."

"So Nelson and Bernie were close, huh?"

"I'd say so. Nelson is the one who gave Bernie his first camera. Also a graduation present," Cook said. "But enough chinwagging. Patty'll be in here soon, and I'd like to be busy enough to ignore her."

I rinsed my mug and brushed away the toast crumbs. Then I headed into the study. Today was dusting and polishing day.

As funny as it sounded, I enjoyed cleaning the study. No one else liked this room, but it was my favorite. I loved how the sun shone through the stained glass, leaving ripples of color on the walls or floor depending on the time of day. I'd even learned to admire the painting of Mr. Thornberry, despite his harsh eyebrows and sharp gaze.

But most of all, the study held the door to the secret garden behind its empty bookshelf. And how could one not love that?

The garden wasn't such a secret now. Miss Janice had surprised me a time or two returning through the hidden door, her cheeks flushed apple pink, and with a fresh joy about her.

I knew it was only time before she'd share that special place with Gerald. I felt oddly jealous over that idea.

I reached for my favorite dusting cloth out of my cleaning basket. Yes, I had a favorite. This cloth was soft and held the dust instead of spreading it into clouds. And my nose was grateful for that.

I cleaned the room until nearly lunchtime, taking my time to polish all the wainscoting, the massive desk, and the bookcase. My heart always clenched at the sight of the empty shelves. Although Miss Janice had changed a lot, she still hadn't warmed up to books yet.

I'd just finished and on my way to the cleaning closet when I heard Patty storm down the stairs.

"Lucy!" she yelled, sounding in the heat of fury.

I abruptly turned right and hurried down the long hallway to the library to get out of her way.

As I approached the great library doors with the wild lion's head, I remembered catching Gerald in there. Why had he been in there, really? Was there something I'd missed?

With that question in mind, I gripped the brass door handles and yanked it open. I had to take another peek.

The room was as spooky as ever. Then I heard the familiar scratching on the wainscoting. I hurried over to pop it open. Apparently, I'd taken too long because Hank stared at me with a bit of disdain that I'd dared tarry.

Of course, I immediately apologized. "Hank, baby! I'm so sorry. Were you in there long?" I rubbed his bumpy spine and then the flagpole of his tail. He swished it from my hands and strolled over to the fireplace.

He gave the hearth a good sniff, and I remembered how he'd been in the room, hissing with his tail puffed out, the day I'd caught Gerald. And hadn't Gerald been standing right where Hank was sniffing now?

I walked over to the hearth and peered into the fireplace. I remembered when I first entered the room I'd seen something in the fireplace, ages ago. But when Miss Janice had caught me and threatened to fire me, I'd forgotten all about it. The ashes looked disturbed now. I grabbed the poker to stir where I remembered seeing a white object. It was gone!

How would Gerald have known it had been in here? Did he pick it out? But why?

I brushed my hands on my skirt before taking a slow circle around the room to examine the area. I wasn't as afraid of being caught in here and fired now. I think I'd earned Miss Janice's trust over the last few months. However, how far would that trust take me if I were to accuse her boyfriend of doing something suspicious? Probably not far.

My attention landed on one of the empty bookshelves. Sitting on the edge was something fluffy—a little dust bunny. Strange. I walked to the other end for the metal ladder and dragged it along the rail. The metal grated like it was screaming for some oil. I reached the shelf and climbed up the metal rails. Leaning in, I peeked at the wood. The dust had been disturbed up here, leaving a clean streak. I held my hand over the mark. It looked like it had been made by someone with larger hands than mine.

The shelf itself was empty, besides the clean smear. Still, I knew how this house worked. Reaching in, I pushed against the back of the shelf. With all the hiding places in this house, nothing would surprise me.

Sure enough, the back board wiggled. I pressed it a few times, and it popped open as if on springs, proving to be a false back. I pulled it out and set it to one side before peering in. Disappointingly, it was empty.

But wait. I saw a disturbance in the dust here as well. I reached for my phone for some light. I still couldn't get a good look. Determined, I brought up the camera to take a picture. It flashed, and I checked the screen.

There in the dust was an outline of a key. It appeared to have once been the hiding space for an ancient skeleton key. There was also a circle shape that looked like it had been made by a coin. Did Gerald know those two items were tucked up in here? How could he?

Or had he been speaking the truth when he said he'd heard Hank? Frowning, I climbed down and shoved the ladder back.

"What are you doing in here?" A near-hysterical whisper erupted from behind me. I about leaped out of my skin as I spun around to look.

It was Janet.

"You scared me," I whispered back, hand over my thumping chest.

"Scared you? I heard a screeching sound from inside this room and about passed out. I had to check to make sure it wasn't ghosts!"

I laughed. "It would be more likely to be rodents."

Her face paled. "That would be so much worse."

She had a point there.

"Shut the door," I said.

Janet turned and pushed it closed. Her eyes opened wide as she studied the room.

"I caught Gerald in here last time he was over," I confessed.

"You did?" Her mouth dropped open. Everyone knew how taboo this room was.

"Yeah. So I came back to figure out what he was doing in here."

"Maybe he was just admiring the…" she vaguely waved to the walls and walls of empty bookshelves. The emptiness was a bit macabre.

"Maybe," I said uncertainly. "The thing is, I found signs of disturbance."

"Like what?"

She'd think I was nuts, but I had to forge on. "Well, months ago, I found something in the fireplace when I first started here. It was white and about this big." I held my fingers a couple of inches apart. "It looked like glass, maybe. But before I could pick it out, Miss Janice came in here and ordered me out. Tonight, when I looked for it, it was gone.

And check this out." I hurried on to my second clue as her eyes began to glaze over with doubt. I thrust out the phone to show her the key photo. This seemed to catch her attention.

She glanced up at the shelves. "That's from up there?"

"Not only up there, but behind a false back."

"How wild." She studied the photo again. "That's a skeleton key, right?"

"Yeah." My attention sharpened. "Does this remind you of anything?"

"Well, I'm sure it's nothing. Never mind."

"What do you mean, never mind?"

"It's dumb."

"I'd never think that. I just told you I was raking through ashes."

She smiled shyly. "I don't know, being the youngest of ten kids, I guess I'm used to not being listened to."

Her wistfulness made me sad. "Anytime you want to talk to someone, I'm here. But even if no one wants to listen, you need to know you are worth being listened to."

She grinned then. "Well, there's this briefcase I know about that has an old-fashioned lock. Marguerite always told me just to leave it alone."

I grinned then. "Show me."

CHAPTER FOURTEEN

*W*e'd hardly taken the second turn past the stairs when Mary found Janet and me. She paused, her arms full of folded sheets, and her eyebrows raised like two antennas zeroing in on a secret.

"Just where are you two going?" she asked. Mary had a way of sniffing out adventure.

Janet shrugged and then gave her sly grin. "Secret mission."

Mary glanced at the sheets in her hand. She moved inside a room and, a moment later, came out empty-handed. "I'm in," she announced emphatically, brushing a curl from her face.

I nodded. The Three Musketeers. Let's do this. "So, where is this case?" I asked Janet.

"Case? What case?" Mary's words arced with curiosity.

"This way," Janet whispered. Her shoes barely made a sound as she stealthily led us down the hallway, past the scowling ancestors. We took the back stairs, a way I rarely ever went. The stairs opened onto the floor with our bedrooms. From there, she led us into her room.

"It's up there." She pointed to a crawlspace above her bed. "That space has always creeped me out."

My gaze darted from the open crawlspace to her face. "What? You're not going?"

She shook her head. "I peeked in there once when Marguerite had me carry up a bag. I swore I'd never go back. Especially not now, after the skeleton in the wall. I hate that it's in my room." She rubbed her arms with a shiver.

"Well, I don't want to go up there either." Mary lowered her bottom lip petulantly. "I'm not exactly fond of cobwebs and dark spaces or skeletons.."

Janet nodded sympathetically.

"What are you guys talking about? Don't you remember I was with you when we found Mr. Bones?" I said.

"Yeah, but you're stronger," Janet said.

"Stronger?" I rolled my eyes. "I know what that compliment means. It means you're trying to mollify me, so I'll get my butt up there."

They grinned like butter wouldn't melt in their mouths.

I shook my head and grabbed her chair, and yanked it over to the opening. "Where's Hank when I need him."

"Why do you want him?" Janet asked.

"He's a great mouse hunter."

Mary winced while Janet ignored my answer. "It's right at the top of the ladder."

I climbed up the chair. Carefully, I lifted the crawl space opening and pushed it back. Then I heaved myself inside.

Of course, the case wasn't at the top like she'd said. After my eyes adjusted, I saw a satchel at the back of the wall space. The old-fashioned brass key lock was visible from the closet lighting filtering through the crack. I wiggled onto my stomach and reached, finally able to loop a finger through the handle of the briefcase and gratefully pulled it out.

I slithered back onto the chair with a thump.

"Wow, impressive," Mary hummed as she took the antique case from me. It really was, the leather embossed with a charming town scene.

"Hurry and shut it!" Janet pointed to the opening. I yanked the board back across. I couldn't blame her. I'd hate to have that in my room as well. I'd seen too many horror flicks to be okay with that.

Mary pressed the latches on the case, but the locks didn't open. She examined the keyhole. "Wish we had the key to it."

"Well, I have this." I showed her the picture of the dusty key imprint. "It's what started the search. But someone stole it."

"Give me a sec," she said, staring at it. Then she plucked out her phone and started violently typing.

"What—?"

She held up a finger to tell us to wait. After a moment, she pressed a button and held the phone to her ear. "Locksmith," she whispered. A second later, someone answered. "Hello? Rudy's Locksmith? I have a weird situation here. I have a locked briefcase, and I have a key imprint. Is there anything you can do with that? Bring the picture down? Okay, got it!"

We left the room, smiling and feeling like we had a new clue.

However, every last bit of the excellent feeling promptly deflated with the sight of Patty standing outside the door, foot tapping.

"What are you three doing? I heard something about Rudy's Locksmith."

"Spare room, ma'am," Mary answered, stepping forward and in the process covering the case in my hands. "Janet heard something in the wall, so we checked the closet for rodents. We thought the door was locked, but it seems all clear."

Patty's eyes narrowed but before she had a chance to respond, Janet jumped in like she'd been tag-teamed. "The wiring has been acting up in that room, so we wanted to be sure everything was safe."

Patty couldn't argue with that, so she simply told us to go about our duties. "Mr. Gerald is here for the afternoon. I want everything to work like clockwork."

We all scattered.

I stopped by my room to drop off the case and then ran down to the kitchen. There Cook rattled off a list of fresh ingredients she needed and sent me to my favorite place on the estate, the herb garden. I didn't have time to tarry today and quickly picked the oregano and thyme, enjoying the sharp scent of freshly picked greens.

Mary was at the sink washing wine glasses when I returned.

"How are we getting to town for the locksmith?" I asked her.

"Patty will never let us," Mary sighed. "Not after our last afternoon off."

"That was a legitimate afternoon off! We didn't do anything wrong. We even hurried back to be sure we were on time."

That did it for Cook. "Oh, she won't, will she? You're allowed time off." Her lips pressed into determined lines. Or were they angry? She threw the dough against the butcher block, and a cloud of flour spun into the air. I took a step back. Definitely angry. I wonder what Patty had done to her recently.

"I need you to go pick up something for me." Her floury hand fished inside her bra and eventually brought out a credit card.

"Take this." She brandished it to me. "Bring me back a bottle of good wine."

I grabbed it gingerly, cringing at the warmth, and then glanced at her for more information.

"I think it will take you a couple of hours." She ended the statement with a question. Mary lifted a shoulder and three fingers. "Three hours, I think. Thank you, and I'll cover for you. Off you go, now."

We ran upstairs to dress in street clothes. On the way back, I gave the chess piece a pat, and we made our way outside. I followed Mary around the garage, and soon we were off.

As we drove, Mary puckered her brow. "I heard from Marguerite."

"You did?" I hadn't realized they were that close. A stab of jealousy went through me.

She turned sad eyes toward me. "She was calling for Cook, and I answered the phone. I don't think she's coming back."

"Seriously?" I'd heard it as a rumor, but hearing it from Mary somehow made it more of a threat.

"She's reconnected with her nephew, Jerry."

It seemed odd to think of her with outside family. We were her family. But of course, she had relationships outside of all of us.

Mary continued, "They hadn't talked for like five years. Something to do with a terrible falling-out between her and her brother."

A brother too? I must have looked confused because Mary glanced at me and nodded. "I know. I was surprised as well. I think they are half-siblings. When their father died, the estate was a mess, and a new will trumped the old one, leaving everything to her brother and step-mom."

"That's horrible!"

"It caused a lot of bad blood between her and her brother, consequently also hurting her relationship with Jerry. But when he found out she was in town, he reached out to her. She said the visit has gone real well. Jerry has his own children now, two twin boys. They could really use Marguerite in their lives."

I grimaced. "Which would leave us with —"

"Patty. It can't get any worse."

The silence between us grew like smog in the city. I couldn't wait to get out of the car, so Rudy's Locksmith sign brought welcome relief. I jumped out after she barely parked, needing fresh air. The thought of being trapped forever with Patty crushed me with a depressive weight. I felt like I could cry.

Maybe I'd go back home and try to find a job there. Mom and Grandma no longer lived at home. They were still staying with Grandma's sister. I'd be alone.

I sighed and glanced up at the building. The shop was on the second floor, just a tiny little hole in the wall. A set of outdoor metal stairs led up there, where several more businesses crowded that level. The other stores looked like a pawn shop and something with guns. I glanced at Mary, who was locking up her car, and then we headed up the stairs.

I pulled up the photo on the phone as we entered the business. The dim interior had no furniture other than a glass counter on which sat a weird-looking machine. A throat clearing had me turn to see a man in an armchair with a book in his hand.

"Can I help you?" he asked.

Mary gave a big smile. "Rudy?"

He nodded. He seemed closed off, as if he were studying us.

"I called you earlier today about making a key for us?"

"That's right." He stood up, causing the chair to creak. It was an old piece, with the upholstered cushion dented to the shape of his body from years of use. He walked forward. And I saw he was quite a bit younger than I realized.

Mary looked at me, and I found the key imprint photo.

"This is what we have." I passed it over. Mary walked to a giant wooden bear carving to examine it.

He brushed his thick hair back from his face and then accepted the phone. He glanced at me again.

"That's the picture of what we need," I clarified.

He looked at it. "This is an oldie, it sure looks like. Only three prongs."

"Can you make one?" Mary leaned against the counter, anxiously.

He nodded. "Yeah. Of course, I can."

Relief flooded through me, and we grinned at each other.

"Only problem is the photo won't help."

"What do you mean?"

"I need to measure things. I can't even tell the size proportions from that photo. I need something to make a template."

I frowned. How could I make a template out of something that a sneeze could ruin?

He seemed to understand I was confused. "Bring in the locked case."

"You can make it from that?" Mary asked.

"Yeah, sure. Here, let me get your name." He posed to write it down on a pad of paper on the counter.

Mary rattled it off. "We'll be back soon."

On the way to the car, I caught Mary shaking her head.

"What's the matter?"

"I swear that guy reminds me of someone."

CHAPTER FIFTEEN

he air felt prickly as Mary drove like a race-car driver trying to get back to the manor.

"You think we have time to leave again?" I asked.

She gritted her teeth. "If we hurry. Cook will cover for us, and it's Lucy's turn to do dinner service." She glanced at me. "You think this briefcase is important?"

I sighed. "I don't know. Bernie left behind a lot of secrets. One of them is probably the reason he ended up killed. I'd like to figure that out, wouldn't you?"

"What drives you to need to know?" she asked.

I stared out the window. The car swooped past the telephone poles. For some reason, a memory of me as a child popped into my head, one where I'd stared out the window and pretended my hand was a chainsaw chopping through each one as my mom took me to school.

"Laura Lee?" Mary prompted.

"There's something about finding Bernie in the wall that fires me up with a sense of injustice. I can't stand that feeling. Lately, it feels like the entire world is one of those tops that once spun perfectly but now is starting to wobble. And the wobble feels like an injustice. I guess I feel if I can fight for something, figure it out, and hold someone accountable, I'm helping to right that wobble."

"And you think you can find Bernie's murderer?" she asked.

"Maybe." I shrugged. "Maybe all the clues are there speaking out about what happened to him. I just want to be careful and listen."

"What kinds of clues do you think we have?"

"Well, the letter for one. And now the briefcase. Nelson the butler, murdered—"

"They didn't deem that as murder, by the way," Mary interrupted.

"What? No! How is that possible? He had the IV line around his neck."

"They say he tried to get up and got tangled in his lines."

CEECE JAMES

The idea made me sick. "No, way. I don't believe it." I cracked the window for fresh air.

She nodded thoughtfully. "Yeah. I don't either."

"I mean, it's always bothered me that Terry knew about his dad's death and didn't show up for work when we drove straight there from the scene."

"Maybe the police informed him before he left." She sighed. "Maybe everything you think is a clue is really weird coincidences."

I bit my thumbnail, considering that.

"Anything else?" she asked.

"Well, there is me finding Gerald in the library and the missing key."

"That could have been a coincidence." Mary tucked back a curl flying in the air from the open window. "He has nothing to gain from any of this."

I nodded. "True. But Hank did not like him."

She snorted. "I don't like him either."

"Why not?"

"Because he's friends with Patty! She makes his special drinky-drink," she said in a high-pitched voice and lifted her pinky finger.

132

We both laughed.

"So, anything else, Miss Sherlock?"

I shrugged. "What about Kenner? Someone hired him."

"Nelson."

"No. Kenner said we needed to figure out who really hired him. And they did hire him to look for something in the library." I could feel my forehead crease. It always tensed like that when I was confused. "Also, the bottle."

"What bottle?"

"The broken glass bottle we found by Bernie. I feel like I should know what it is."

"Oh, that. I know what it was."

I turned to her. "Seriously? It's been bugging me all this time."

"Sure. It's an old milk bottle."

Something flickered in my mind, telling me that was important. But, by now, she had turned into the driveway and crept up to the garage to park.

"Come on, let's hurry," she said and jetted out. We hurried around the manor and through the back door. The door slammed behind us, making me wince at our ruined silent return.

"Wait a minute, Mary!"

"What?" She turned to me as Jessie walked up.

"The person who broke into the house was supposed to be the milkman's son. That night on Halloween. Supposedly it was a prank."

Before she had a chance to answer, Jessie interrupted. "Where've you guys been?"

"We had an errand to run, and we're actually still on our way," Mary answered in a rush. "I forgot something."

Jessie dismissed Mary with a wave and pointed at me. "Something came to the house for you today. I put it up in your room."

"Oh?" I couldn't imagine who would send me something. Not my mom. She was on a tight income and didn't even own a cell phone. She claimed she didn't need much, that good health and a happy family made her the richest woman in the world. Since she was recovering from an illness, I could well appreciate her sentiments. Her health made me feel the same way.

So who else would have sent me a package?

I bounded up to my room to get the suitcase. Jessie had set the plain cardboard box a few inches inside the door. It was addressed to me, but the return address had been smudged, perhaps touched while the ink was still wet.

I sat on the floor to open it. Hank must have heard me enter because the cabinet door cracked open. He walked in with his back arched in a good stretch, and he yawned, pink tongue curled. Then his pupils tightened as he zeroed in on the box.

Instantly his personality changed. Ears pointing forward, he stalked over. He sniffed the corner. There was something about it he didn't like, and he quickly backed away, mouth open.

Of course, that put me on edge, especially not being able to read the smear to see who it was from. Cautiously, I grabbed a nail file to break the packing tape.

I'd hardly peeled it back when a noxious odor escaped from inside. I pushed the box away as Hank hissed. The hair on his neck raised like a porcupine ruff. I thought the cat would disappear back into the wall, but he hung in there with me.

A gentle tap came from the door. I jumped, startled, and then called out, "Come in!"

Mary stuck her face in, her eyes wide with excitement. "You ready?"

"Check this out." I pushed the box toward her. She'd hardly taken a step in before she pinched her nose. "Wow, that stinks. What's going on in here?"

"Someone sent it to me."

"This is what Jessie meant? Some kind of joke? Get it out of here!" She nudged the box with her foot, and it tipped over with a clunk. Dead beetles spilled out, along with a fish head.

Mary gasped. "Is that what I think it is?"

I nudged them back inside with my foot. "We're taking this with us."

"Taking? We? In my car?"

"We need to make a stop at the police department."

"I don't think they'll care."

"It's not a joke. This is a threat."

Mary held the box shut with her foot. "Get some tape."

I rushed through my drawer and grabbed some tape and fastened the box shut. She lifted the briefcase. I nervously picked up the box, and we headed back downstairs. We snuck down the stairs when we heard Patty screech from the other room, "Where is that housemaid?"

"Hurry," Mary whispered.

We raced as fast as one can on tiptoe out the front door. Mary disappeared through. Butler eyed me, and I smiled disarmingly before giving a glance around. The coast was clear.

"Butler, can I ask you a question?"

He straightened and gave me a disapproving look. "Miss Patty is bound to come through soon."

Miss Patty. Ugh. Her very name made my stomach twist. "I'll make it quick. Did you happen to know old Butler?"

"Not him necessarily, but his son."

"Terry? How did you know him?"

"We went to school together, years ago." His eyes softened, showing crinkles at their corners.

"You were friends then?"

"Not friends exactly. Schoolmates. I hardly hung out with most of that crowd. They left for college, and I found a job in a shoe factory."

"It seems like you think of Terry favorably."

He shook his head. "He was a scamp. Always getting into trouble. And make sure you knew where you left your stuff around him. He'd steal anything not nailed down."

"Cook!" Patty screeched from somewhere down the hall.

Butler blanched. "You better go," he suggested.

I nodded and ran out the door. I found Mary already in the driver's seat and dumped the box in the trunk she'd left open.

"Where to first?" Mary asked, putting the car into gear with a clunk.

"Definitely the police station," I answered, snapping on my seatbelt.

"I don't think they're going to believe us," Mary said, pushing the code for the gate to open again. It opened slowly with shudders and left long black striped shadows across the ground. A striped shadow crossed her face.

"Let's try anyway," I answered.

She drove us to the police station, where it took us almost as long to find a parking spot as it did to get there. Finally, she jockeyed into a space, giving me both anxiety and admiration since the spot was so tight.

We were met by someone at the front desk when we walked inside. "How can I help you?" she asked.

"I'm not sure," I answered, setting the box on the counter.

Her eyebrows rose with alarm. "Can you please remove that?" she said, gesturing with her pen.

I grabbed it and glanced around, unsure where to put it, before setting it by my feet. "I received this package in the mail. I think it's a threat, and I'm not sure who to report it to."

"What's in the box?" she asked. "Did you open it?"

"Yes. I saw a bunch of dead beetles and fish."

"Did you see anything mechanical?" she asked.

"I didn't open it all the way to find out."

It occurred to me what she was thinking. The box contained a bomb. In a professional, calm tone, she called for someone to report to the front desk.

Almost immediately, two police officers bustled out from the background. One wore a shirt that obviously covered a bulletproof vest in the way it tightly buttoned over a square shape. The other young officer had jittery energy like this was his first day on the job.

The older one squinted at me. "I'm Officer Daniels. What have you got? Some kind of bomb?" He looked suspiciously at the box at my feet.

"I'm not sure what it is. The box came in the mail and has dead bugs and stuff in it. I'm concerned because it came anonymously."

He stared at the scotch tape sealing the top.

"We retaped it," I explained.

With one finger, he pulled up in the flap to peek inside. I heard something rattle around. He grunted and then lifted the box. By his confidence in handling it, I felt sure it was not a bomb.

"Come on back and join me," he said over his shoulder. I glanced at Mary, unsure if he meant both of us, but she took matters into her own hands and started after him anyway, leaving me behind.

He took us to his desk, where he left the box to one side and opened up his computer.

"Your name?" he asked.

I gave it, and also my contact information.

"You know anybody who would want to send you something as a prank?"

The word *prank* made my eyebrows spike up. I answered, "No."

He typed laboriously for a few minutes, driving me crazy as his finger solidly planted across the keys. The young officer returned with a cup of coffee. Officer Daniels glanced up and seemed surprised to see we were still there.

"You can go now. I'll let you know if I learn anything about this. Most of this stuff turns out to be a harmless prank. I wouldn't worry about it."

Dismissed, Mary and I headed back out of the precinct and into the bright, stabbing sunlight.

"Well, what did I tell you?" Mary asked, tugging on a pair of sunglasses.

"Right as usual," I answered a little glumly.

She gave a big grin. "What's that?"

"You heard me," I said as she laughed and climbed into the car. Mary liked to be right, that's for sure.

As she backed out, she asked, "What do you think we're going to do if Patty stays?"

"I think Miss Janice is going to have a retreat on her hands. I don't think half the staff will continue to work there. Especially Cook. So she'll be forced to find a new head housekeeper."

"I highly doubt that." Mary's eyebrows rumpled. "Cook talks a big game, but she has nowhere else to go. This is her family, and Miss Janice too. You know she's lived here for almost her whole life. I am assuming she plans on staying, and Miss Janice will let her retire here so she can sit in the kitchen and watch the new cook with an eagle eye."

I sighed, feeling discouraged. That was my last hope.

"Besides, Cook doesn't answer to Patty," Mary said, turning on her blinker.

I rested with my chin in my hand and my elbow on the armrest and stared out the window. I guess I was going to have to endure it too. Jobs were tight, and this one paid me good money. Mom and grandma were finally getting back on their feet. After that, I needed to hit my school loans. I was in no position to go back to a low-paying job and have to pay for rent and food.

We drove silently for a while, both of us discouraged, I think. Eventually, she turned into the locksmith's building again. I scooped up the briefcase and we ascended the stairs to the tiny little office again.

After all that trouble, it was a little disconcerting to see a little white sign on the door that read, closed.

Mary's forehead rumpled. "What do you mean, closed?"

I glanced at the time. Two o'clock. "Do you think he's gone for lunch?"

"I'm not sure."

At just that moment, an older gentleman climbed the stairs. He smiled at us when he reached the top. "Can I help you?" he asked, slightly breathless.

"We're just waiting for the Locksmith to open again. Do you know where he is? We were here earlier looking for a key to be made," Mary said.

He frowned. "That's impossible."

"Why?" I asked.

His thin gray hair fluttered in the breeze. "Because this is my business, and it's the first time I've been here all day."

CHAPTER SIXTEEN

"Pardon me?" Mary's eyebrows lifted so high she looked like she wore a jester mask.

"I'm Rudy, and this is my shop."

"It wasn't opened earlier?" I asked.

The older man glanced at us with a worried expression of someone who had been robbed before. He shuffled toward the door with a key extended in his shaky hand. "I never come in before having lunch with the missus. She's been wanting me to retire for years. It's her rule that we never miss a meal if I keep working." Some of his good humor returned, and his eye twinkled. "And I tell you what, I don't want to miss a meal. So what's that about you already being here?"

"We talked on the phone, and you told us to come down. I swear, we were right inside your business not two hours ago. You have a wooden bear in there."

His eyes locked on hers with concern. "Well, I remember our phone call. All calls are forwarded to my cell at home. But I'm telling you, I wasn't here." The door finally unlocked, and he opened it with a soft nudge. He hesitated a second, studying the interior, before taking a cautious step forward. His head swiveled, checking to make sure nothing was disturbed.

"Right here," Mary moved past him. "I left my information on a pad...." She trailed off, and I knew what she'd found. The desk was empty.

"What's there?" He limped over, his shoes softly scuffling against the boards.

"The information the other man took."

He shook his head. "I'm not sure what you mean. I keep everything on the computer. It's the 21st century, you know."

I couldn't help my smile, especially when he pulled out an antique pocket watch to check the time. I half-expected a monocle to come out along with it. He examined the strange-looking machine and his blanks, and then joggled an antique cash register until it opened. Satisfied, he shut it, making the register's bell ding.

Rudy rubbed his freshly shaven cheeks, the skin slightly red from the scrape of the razor. "Well, everything seems in order. I'm not sure what that was all about, but what was it you needed?"

Mary stared as if surprised at his casualness at discovering a stranger had been in his business. Her shoulders slumped as she gave up. "We needed a key made. We came in with a photo of it, but the man (here she stressed the word *man*) said he needed the actual case to see the size."

"Oh?" His thin eyebrows bundled up and blended in with the road map of wrinkles on his forehead. "Let me see it, then."

Mary put the briefcase on the counter while I searched my phone for the key's image.

His rough hand reached out for the case to examine the lock. I noticed his fingernails had ridges, and they were long and thick. Then he looked at my picture and gave a pleased little snort.

"I know what this is. I don't even need the case to be able to make this key. This is a number twenty-two skeleton key, made for many things, including cases like this. Whose case is it?"

I hesitated, wondering how to start the story off, but, as usual, Mary came to my rescue. "It's my grandma's," she said with a confident smile. "We found the case and, as you can see from the imprint in the dust, there was a key laying next to it. We're hoping that you can open the case for us."

Rudy walked to the rear, where a wall glittered from blank keys hung on a board. From underneath a desk, he pulled out a metal box. Grunting, he lifted it onto the counter. He flipped the latches, and it opened to reveal an interior filled to the brim with rattling keys. His rough fingers riffled through, pulling first this key and then that to hold up to the light to examine it. Finally, he found one that made him happy. He checked my picture again and then walked over with slow shuffling steps to our case and pressed the key into the lock.

Nothing happened. He didn't give up, though. Instead, he jiggled the key in and out and gently turned it. Within a second, the case clicked open.

Mary and I both giggled at the sound of the click. Rudy looked quite pleased with himself. He handed Mary the key.

"That'll be 14.50," he said in his growly voice.

Mary pulled out the debit card. He passed it carefully through the machine and then handed it back.

Meanwhile, both Mary and I stared greedily at the case. We couldn't wait to see inside but didn't want to open it in front of him. Mary raised an eyebrow at me, and I nodded. She reached over and latched it shut again with a click.

"Thank you so much." She smiled. "You saved something special. I don't know what we would've done without you."

Rudy smiled. "Now, what was this about somebody being in my store?"

Mary went on to explain the man that we saw. "Do you have a surveillance video? Maybe you can find them."

He shuffled back to his computer. "I do have surveillance. The missus demanded I put it in a few years back. We had a break-in, and she said that to keep working I had to have a spy camera."

"And come home for meals," I added with a smile.

He chuckled softly. "Yes, that's right. Now let's see what we can find on that." He clicked the computer to bring up the video. After a moment, the lines on either side of his mouth deepened in displeasure. "It seems like someone's messed with my darn camera." He walked over to the corner where the camera was located. He grunted with disapproval.

"What's the matter?" I asked.

"Someone sprayed my camera lens with black paint," he growled. "Don't they know how expensive that is?"

"Maybe you need to call the police," Mary suggested.

"I just might do that," he nodded.

With one last thank you, Mary waved her hand in goodbye as I pocketed the key and lifted the briefcase.

I stared up at the camera on my way out. It gave me the shivers. I couldn't help but notice it was directly above the worn leather chair where we'd met the first man. Who was he, and what had we walked into?

CHAPTER SEVENTEEN

I have to admit, my heart was racing by the time we made it down the stairs. Mary placed the suitcase on the backseat.

"Should I do it?" Her fingers trembled on the latch. I handed her the key.

She looked at me and smiled and jabbed it vigorously into the lock.

"Wait!" I stopped her as a premonition sent tickles along the little hairs on my neck.

"What's wrong?" Mary asked.

"What if the guy who pretended to be the locksmith is still here someplace, watching us?"

"That's ridiculous," she scoffed. "He had no idea we were coming here. That was just a coincidence. He had nothing to do with us."

I nodded, but something didn't strike me as right. "He was awful curious about the briefcase." I touched the embossing with a finger. "He wanted us to bring it in. Why would he do that? Besides, remember how you thought you'd seen him before?"

Mary shrugged. "I don't know. Who knows why people do what they do. Maybe he was curious, too." But I noticed her finger quit turning the key.

"Why don't we at least do this someplace else safe," I suggested.

She nodded reluctantly and shut the door. I walked around and got into the passenger seat.

"Where's someplace safe?" she asked, belting herself in.

I hesitated. I didn't want to try and drag this case into the house without knowing what was in it. "Maybe the park?" I asked

She nodded and started the car. Soon we were headed down the highway with the wind blowing our hair as the open windows let in fresh air. My heart bubbled with that light excitement that happens when something good is coming.

Mary, however, did not seem as lighthearted.

"What's the matter?" I asked.

She glanced into the rearview mirror. "Nothing," she said. "Or maybe something."

"That gives me absolutely zero information," I retorted.

She stepped on the gas and sped up before glancing into the rearview mirror again. "It's just that the red car that was parked next to us earlier seems to be following us."

"Okay." I felt alarmed. "But, before we panic, if they're on this highway, doesn't it just mean they're probably heading back to town, too?

"Could be."

I notice she still sped up.

Then she grimaced. "However, when I change lanes, that car changes lanes as well."

To experiment, she changed three lanes over as if she were taking the next exit. I watched out the back window.

"Look, see?" I said, relieved. "He's staying in the far left lane. It was just a coincidence."

Just then, the car's blinker turned on. I shouted, "You're totally right."

She pressed her lips together grimly as her hands clenched the wheel. The car in front of us quickly slowed. As their brake lights flashed, I squealed, and Mary stamped on the brakes. Immediately I glanced over my shoulder. The red car had slowed as well.

My tongue felt dry. Fear can do strange things to a person. Make them stronger, weaker, or dry their tongue out like a little autumn leaf. "Mary, what are we going to do?"

"Don't worry. I was always the driver when we were teenagers, and I got out of a speeding ticket more than once by knowing how to get away."

I glanced at her, even more alarmed. I didn't know if I was more afraid of her crazy driving or the guy behind us.

Immediately Mary stepped on the gas and swerved into the left lane without using her signal.

I screamed while she raced down the road, engine roaring. She swooped down the next exit, with me squealing the whole time.

The red car zoomed past, still stuck on the highway.

"You, my friend, are a rock star," I shouted.

Mary grinned from ear to ear.

"Now, let's go find a private spot to figure out what is in this briefcase."

After a few more turns, she pulled over in a park behind a housing development.

"My aunt used to live in here," she said, explaining how she knew the location of the park.

Kids filled the crowded playground, but she found a shady spot under some tall trees. She parked the car, and we both hurried out and around to the back passenger side.

"So, you ready?" she asked.

I gave the area a quick look-over. No one seemed to care about us over here. "Yeah," I answered, a little nervous still. It felt like the red car could show up any minute. "But hurry."

She jabbed the key into the lock and twisted it. After giving it a few jiggles, as the locksmith had, the lock clicked, and the lid popped up a quarter of an inch.

Nervous energy filled the air. She licked her lips and pushed the lid up all the way. Anxiously, we both stared inside.

There was an envelope at the bottom.

"All this for a crummy letter?"

"It might be a will. Have some faith." I picked it up and turned it over in my hand.

It was a very old envelope. The hair on my arms prickled when I saw it was sealed with a wax stamp.

"Do we dare break it?" I asked.

She held up her hand. "Wait a second." With that, she dove for her purse between the front seats. After a moment, I heard a satisfied grunt, and she came back with fingernail clippers. In a flash, she flipped them open and slid out a tiny nail file.

"This will work like a letter opener and save the wax seal," she explained and took the letter from me. With a clever stab, she worked the silver point into the top of the envelope and soon had it opened.

"There!" she said, passing it back to me proudly.

"Great idea. The seal might be another clue, and I'm glad we didn't destroy it." Carefully, I slid out the flimsy piece of paper.

The paper had no writing. Instead, wrapped inside a thin sheet of tissue paper, was a photograph.

The photograph was of two people in front of a school. A man and a woman. I flipped it over and saw the names D. and M. Escott.

CHAPTER EIGHTEEN

We both stared at the picture. "You think this is one of Bernie's photographs?" Mary asked.

"It has to be." I flipped it over to see if there was writing on it and then went back to examine the briefcase. I felt the sides and bottom, but they seemed solid.

"You're thinking there's a false bottom?"

"Maybe."

"Let's get it home before we start tearing it apart," she suggested. I nodded.

When we got home, I immediately headed into the kitchen. "Here's your credit card back. I'm so sorry, but we forgot the wine."

Cook stood before a pot of bubbling water. "Did you girls get your errand done?" she asked. She opened a bag of macaroni noodles, in the process sending several into the air. She poured the contents into the water. After a moment, she plucked a dried noodle out of her bra and threw it into the pot.

"Some of them," I answered. "We had to go to the police station."

Lucy came in then, appearing wiped out.

"You okay?" I asked.

She shrugged and found a spoon. Seconds later, she dug out a mound of peanut butter and then replaced the container in the pantry.

"Why the police?" Cook asked. "You stopped at the important part."

I explained the weird box, and she shook her head, her eyes horrified.

"Up in your room, you say? Dead fish heads?"

Lucy shivered.

"And dead beetles. Hank freaked out." I thought about how he stuck around instead of slipping back through the crack. "He stayed with me though."

"That cat is something else. You know how we came by Hank, don't you?"

"No. I've always wondered," I said.

"That's a story to tell." Cook stirred the pot and added salt.

The kitchen door slammed back, and Patty stormed in. Her eyes narrowed when she saw me. "Where have you been?"

Cook interrupted. "They were doing a shopping errand for me. Besides, all the chores are done, and these girls are two of the best. Why are you so bothered?"

Patty bristled like an angry sleep-deprived chicken. "I have a reputation to keep up, and I want things to run like clockwork."

"And just what reputation is that?" Cook prodded.

Patty opened her mouth, but I could see she didn't want to answer. Instead, she zeroed in on Lucy. "Are you eating again?"

Lucy's eyes went big. "Why?"

"I like to see you working. And moving a spoon of peanut butter to your mouth isn't working." With that, she marched out.

"You just ignore her, Lucy. She's trying to defend herself, that's all." Cook nodded. "I think this is the first time for her to hold a position this high."

"Why do you say that?" I asked.

"Because any housekeeper worth their salt has worked with their share of stinkers and knows to respect good, hard workers. They're a rare treasure. And that's all of you girls for sure."

I practically glowed from the compliment.

Tonight was my time to turn down Miss Janice's bedroom for nighttime, which also included concocting her sleeping tonic and filling the tub. I wanted to get in and get out. Sometimes she wanted to talk. At certain times, she saw us as friends— paid friends who were meant to listen to her. And I did listen usually. But tonight, I could barely wait to get to the book club and talk about what Mary and I had learned.

Luckily for me, tonight she didn't feel chatty, and after laying out her dressing gown she dismissed me.

I had an hour to go until book club, so I lay on my bed with my sketch pad. I'd left it open to Miss Janice's boyfriend, and looking at it now, I was reminded of Mary's comment about how the guy from the locksmith store had seemed familiar. I studied the slick-backed hair swoop. The hairline did look familiar.

Mary showed up soon after. Wearing striped pajamas and her curly hair in two pigtails, she brought to mind my first babysitting job. That five-year-old had been the female version of Dennis the Menace. I had vivid memories of her sitting on the freezer in defiance of bedtime, finding her dinner tucked behind the couch, and frantically plunging the toilet she'd clogged with her tea set.

"Why are you looking at me like that?" Mary asked.

I grinned. "You reminded me of someone. Speaking of that, today you said the locksmith guy reminded you of someone."

She nodded.

"Was it his hair swoop?"

Her nose wrinkled in thought. "Maybe."

"Take a gander at this." I lifted the sketch pad.

"Gerald?"

I nodded. "About thirty years younger."

"Wow. Weird, right?"

We snuck down the hallway to the club room and sat in our chairs. The mood felt somber. To be honest, something had been off with the group ever since Marguerite had been gone. We were more hushed, more reserved, as if we feared Patty might break into the secret book club room at any moment. It made me sad to think about what would happen if Marguerite didn't come back.

Cook lifted the book we'd been reading this month—*All Creatures Great and Small*—and we went through our thoughts on it. Discussion moved like molasses because every few minutes, our conversation became derailed by crazy topics.

Finally, Cook appeared to give up on the book. She caught my eye. "Laura Lee, did you have something to share?"

With a glance at Mary, who nodded, I walked to the front of the room. "So we found a briefcase, and after a whole bunch of trouble we discovered a picture inside."

Of course, that caused a massive stir of comments from everyone. Questions bombarded me from where we'd found the briefcase (which I ignored) to what kind of trouble I'd gotten into (which I blurred over) all shot at me like fireworks. I waved my hands to quiet everyone down.

Fortunately, it worked.

I brought up the envelope and passed it around. "In the end, this is what we found. Does anyone know anything about this?"

It was passed around with the reverence of holding a golden ticket. Cook took it from Lucy and examined the photo.

"I know who this guy is." She tapped the man on the right. "David Jenson. He was kind of smitten with me, I thought." Cook added thoughtfully.

David Jenson. Had I heard that name before? "Does he still live around here?"

CATASTROPHE IN THE LIBRARY

"He left years ago. Nearly the same time as Bernie."

"But no one thought that was suspicious?"

She shook her head. "Everyone knew his manuscript had been stolen on the ship ride home. He was naturally devastated and needed space to heal."

"What's that in the background?" asked Janet.

Lucy leaned over her shoulder. "Looks like a street sign."

"Any you've seen before?" I asked.

Mary had her phone out and thumbs flying over the keyboard. "Is this one the same?" She held out the phone.

I took it and compared it. It was a street sign from Ireland. "Wow! Good job. How'd you find it?"

"I remembered Bernie and David had just returned from there."

Duh. I cringed. "Perfect sense."

"So, it seems just as obvious that the photo was taken by Bernie. After all, he was the photographer on that trip. But why did he lock this up so tightly?"

Cook shrugged. "I'm not sure who the woman is. Although I'm sure she's close to David."

"How so?" Mary asked. "She looks like she's wearing some type of uniform."

"David thought he was the cat's pajamas when it came to women. He sure couldn't handle rejection, though. So if she's with him, they're close."

"He couldn't handle rejection well?" Those words chilled me.

She nodded. "He liked the girl I replaced."

Replaced didn't sound like a good word. "What happened to her?"

"He didn't know the word no. She was afraid and left before things could get worse."

"And this was Bernie's best friend?" I asked, incredulous.

She lifted her shoulder sadly. "It was a different world in those days."

Jessie asked me, "So, what did you find out about during your visit with Nelson? I mean, other than he's dead."

"His son, Terry, was always no good," Cook sucked her front teeth and frowned.

"You knew him?" Lucy asked.

"Of course, I knew him. He was friends with Bernie and David, so I saw him a time or two, but then after school they all went their separate ways. He stayed here while the other two went to Ireland."

"I'm surprised Bernie had so few friends."

"And why is that?" Cook asked.

"Because you said that when you came back from the quarantine, the manor had been destroyed. That you'd thought he had a huge party?"

Cook frowned. "That's a good point, now that you mention it. He never really was one for big parties. And with him and Terry fighting—" She lifted a finger. "Although I do know for a fact they reconnected after Bernie returned home. I think Bernie tried to make amends. Sadly, it seems it was too little, too late."

"How did you know that?"

"My mother saw Bernie at the dairy. Both he and Terry had walked off together. It was an unusual sight, so she shared it with me."

Mary and I looked at each other. This mystery was becoming stranger and more twisted.

CHAPTER NINETEEN

he next day Miss Janice planned to leave for a dinner party hosted by the town's mayor. Every part of the manor seemed to buzz with her preparations. A whole glam squad commandeered Miss Janice's bedroom suite.

Gerald planned to accompany her to dinner. This would be their first time out as a couple, and every detail needed excruciating attention.

Everything felt even more topsy-turvy and out of sorts because Cook, Janet, Jessie, and Lucy all had their monthly night off. Usually, we never left for the entire evening, but on this night, the girls departed in droves. I think Patty was the catalyst for this, and it left just Mary and me to hold the fort.

Of course, Butler remained behind, rattling around in his quarters. Patty was here someplace as well, although I couldn't be bothered to find out for sure. And Stephen, with Sophia his sister, out in their little cottage. However, I couldn't deny how isolated and quiet the manor felt with its many empty bedrooms.

I took a thick sandwich and a large glass of soda to my room. After taking a big bite, I gathered my sketch pad, phone, and the picture and letter and climbed up on my bed.

The ancient house settled with its usual nighttime groans, sounding like a Grandpa trying to ease himself down in his Fatboy chair. Old joints moaned, boards squeaked and popped as the nighttime temperatures lifted off the warmth of the day.

I remembered then the pictures I'd taken of Nelson's letter at the hospital. It seemed absurd that I'd forgotten, but so much had happened since then. I clicked through the photos and zoomed in.

The letter came from his son, Terry. They seemed sweet and ordinary, and I felt uncomfortable reading them even though they didn't reveal anything more personal than what someone had for lunch and how Terry's butcher business prospered. I recognized the same swirly P that Cook had pointed out that Bernie had also used and comforted myself that I was trying to find out what happened to the both of them.

My email dinged. I logged in, and excitement zinged through me to see that the school had messaged me back. They sent me a link regarding the yearbook. But, as I hovered over the link, I saw my old boyfriend's unanswered emails, and Chris's face that day at the nursing home swam in my memory. I owed him an explanation, didn't I?

Sighing, I brought up Chris's email. My heart hurt to read his confusion. I wanted to say the right thing that might make it better. Then again, he really hadn't seemed that bothered when I saw him in the elevator.

I realized it didn't matter to me, even if he was better. I owed him an explanation regardless.

Dear Chris,

I hope you will get these even after such a late date. I had thought this account was not in use and only received your emails today. And I felt terrible when I saw the news they contained.

First of all, I am so sorry to hear about your grandfather. I know how close you two were, and how much you cherished him, and he you.

I went on to share some specific memories I remember they shared. I ended with another apology, as well as a congratulations and well-wishes for his new job.

Satisfied, I hit send. What would be, would be.

Hank jumped on my bed. In his mouth, he carried something. Weird. What was this? I spread it out and saw a

166

handkerchief. It had black soot smudges on the soft surface, which I recognized even before I saw the initials in the corner. GDH. Could that stand for Gerald Hawkings? It had to.

I picked off a piece of roast beef and offered it to Hank. He sniffed it and then curled his body into a cinnamon roll right on my pillow. I ignored him. After first pretending not to be interested in the food, he nibbled it as soon as he saw I wasn't watching.

I spread the handkerchief flat and saw a strange imprint. I held it up to the light. The ash held an impression of something small.

Hank pressed his feet against me, his toe-beans stretching out. He was surprisingly strong. I squished against the wall to avoid disturbing him and took another bite of my sandwich.

Okay, finally time to hit pay dirt. I tapped the link for the yearbook. It steadily loaded, and I smiled with anticipation.

A thud sounded out in the hallway.

What was that? My spine straightened as I stared at the door. The box of dead beetles and fish heads flashed through my mind. Especially its ill intent.

Mary poked her head into the room. The warm flood of relief made me breathe in deep.

She nibbled on a cookie as she came in and jumped on my bed. "I tell you what, Laura Lee, I'm exhausted. Weary of watching a grown woman run around and cause drama where there doesn't need to be any." Mary's eyes fluttered closed.

"Miss Janice?" I asked, confused.

"Patty." The word dropped from her mouth like a stone.

I nodded. "I wish Miss Janice saw it."

"She doesn't care about things like that. I don't even think she cares about us anymore. Besides, she likes Patty now."

I lifted a shoulder but didn't want to comment. I remembered a time when Miss Janice bought me two dresses so I'd have something pretty. "She's just busy with Gerald. And who can blame her? She's spent a long time alone, and it's nice to have a companion."

Mary nodded. "I guess so. But I wish Marguerite would come back." She glanced over. "What are you doing, anyway?"

"Just trying to put the pieces together." I hesitated and then blurted out. "So I have a theory I want to go over with you."

"What's that?"

This might shock her, but I continued. "I think it was Terry Morgan who killed Bernie."

"Why would he kill his friend?"

"Ex-friend. They had a falling out because Terry thought Bernie's family was ripping off his dad. Terry accused Bernie of being a thief and withholding from Nelson. Cook said when Bernie returned from Ireland, he visited the dairy to meet with Terry and try to patch things up."

"It must not have worked if you think Terry killed him."

"Exactly. I think Terry followed Bernie home, and they fought. That's why the manor was so messed up when the family returned from quarantine. When Bernie tried to hide in the tunnels, Terry followed him in there. He killed Bernie with a milk bottle."

"Just one question." She bounced the bed, making Hank lift his head. He glared at her with the fur on one of his cheek rumpled. "Oops, sorry, your highness," she said, stroking his back. He stared a second longer to show her he was serious before nestling back to sleep. "What motive would Terry have to follow Bernie back?"

"Maybe he knew Bernie had brought some type of treasure. He always felt his dad deserved more money."

"And Terry didn't find it."

"No. Instead, at a later date, he had hired some milkman from work to break the window. And then he suggested Kenner to his dad as a good handyman. Kenner searched for it but was caught by Nelson and escorted out."

"So you're saying no-one found the treasure."

I nodded. "That's what I believe."

"You don't think it was someone else? Maybe Bernie told other friends about what he brought back."

I held up my phone. "Maybe so. I just received the link to check out Bernie's yearbook. It's the closest thing I have before he disappeared, so I wanted to see at least if I could find another link. Want to check it out?"

"Definitely."

I loaded up the yearbook from the link. It opened to the cover.

"Wow, impressive," Mary said, leaning in to look.

Slowly I scrolled through the pages, going faster when I realized the seniors had a huge class that year. Eventually, I found Bernie Thornberry.

I sucked in my breath. The portrait downstairs did him no justice. He was absolutely a handsome guy, and I could see why Cook had, as she called it, "the vapors."

"What do you think?" I asked. "Is he vaporlicious?"

Mary took the phone. "Huh. That's him. Weird. He's cute."

"Yep."

"It says here he was in the chess club." Instead of giving my phone back, Mary continued to scroll.

"That makes sense. I remember Cook telling me he used to play chess with Nelson. What are you looking for?"

"I want to see if there are any pictures of this club." She scrolled in silence for a while, her forehead wrinkled in concentration. She paused. "I don't believe it."

"Believe what?" I practically knocked heads with her trying to see.

"Look who's there." She pointed.

It was a black and white picture of two boys locked into a game of chess. Bernie stared at the pieces while his opponent looked at the camera and smiled.

"You recognize him?"

I studied the young man. Glasses. Dark hair swooped off his forehead. Also very handsome. "I'm not sure."

"How about the guy that met us at the locksmith shop earlier."

I gasped. "You're right!" I lunged for my sketch pad, and we compared the two pictures. My drawing wasn't an exact likeness, however I had managed to capture the swoopiness in Gerald's black hair.

"I have goosebumps," Mary said. She rubbed her arms as if to prove it.

"How can this be? Gerald is not from here," I said in imitation of his accent.

The boy was not named in the photo. The caption simply stated, "Bernie moves his knight."

Cook once mentioned David Jenson as Bernie's other friend. On a hunch, I looked up David.

"We have a winner," I whispered. It was the same person. The author friend who went missing soon after Bernie disappeared. The one Cook had said was handsy and wouldn't take no for an answer.

CHAPTER TWENTY

*M*ary popped the last of her cookie in her mouth and eyed my empty soda glass. "I'll be right back. I need to get a drink. You want anything?"

"More cookies, if you see some."

"You've got it."

She jumped up and left, leaving the door open. It was kind of creepy having my cozy room exposed to the dark unknown of the hallway. I didn't like it, that was for sure.

I leaned over my phone and studied the yearbook chess picture again. Something about it bothered me. On a hunch, I texted Stephen. It was late, but one thing I liked about Stephen was that he never seemed to tire of my questions or think they were dumb.

Quickly, I typed, —**Did your dad ever mention how Bernie played chess?**

I was surprised and happy to see him type back. —**Sure. Both him and his brother played.**

—**I found a picture of him playing chess with David.**

—**Yeah. I believe that.**

I typed my out-of-the-blue question. —**Do you think there is any chance at all that Gerald really is David?**

Instead of waiting for a response, I sent David's yearbook picture. Stephen sent back a shocked face.

My email dinged. Chris had messaged me back. I hardly knew how to switch gears to read it, but I did.

He wrote, "It was good to see you the other day. You think we could grab a cup of coffee and catch up?"

I smiled. It would be good to talk for a bit.

Or would it? I decided to wait a hot minute before I responded. One drama at a time.

I heard movement on the stairs and expected Mary to show up at my door any minute. What was taking her so long?

I spread out the handkerchief again and tried to figure out what would have made the imprint. It kind of looked like the object was around two inches in height. Then it hit me. If I saw something in the fireplace and wanted to grab it, how would I?

Use a handkerchief, of course, if I had one. And I clearly remembered seeing something in the fireplace ashes a long time ago.

I spread the corner flat and studied the initials again.

GDH. Gerald *David* Hawkings. That was it! Gerald had to be David!

Chilled, I glanced back at the chess picture. *Bernie moves his knight.* I lunged for the letter and reread it. Then I typed in the search bar, "How does a knight move in chess?"

The answer came immediately. Three steps forward and two sideways.

Just like the letter.

The hair rose on my neck. Bernie had been referring to a knight. And where did I know there was a knight?

The statue on the stairs.

I jumped up, jiggling the bed enough to make Hank jostle and meow, and grabbed my robe. Then I ran out the door.

The dark hallway seemed blacker than usual and creepily reminded me of the tunnels. Halfway down the slick wood hallway, I realized it would have been helpful if I'd brought my phone with me for light.

I heard a slam downstairs. Mary must've been back on her way upstairs. Geez, she'd taken long enough to drink a gallon.

I returned to my room and seized my flashlight, giving it a click to test it. The light sputtered orange and then blinked off. I smacked it against my palm. It blazed with light, so I relaxed. With my first step in the hallway, it died again.

Seriously?

I whacked it a few more times. The heavy batteries rattled, but it didn't turn back on. A few choice words rolled up my tongue, but I bit them back. Instead, I returned for my cell phone.

Only seven-percent battery left. Terrific. Still, it would hold me until Mary returned.

With the cell flashlight on, I headed out. It did a good enough job brightening the hallway and banishing the ghosties, as Cook would say. The cool wood floor made me wish I'd put on socks, but for Pete's sake I wasn't going back again.

I found the stairwell easily, although I couldn't help but wonder at the lack of lights. Why had the ladies turned everything off when they left? It sure hadn't made things easy for me. I traveled down the two floors, assuming I'd meet Mary on her way back up.

The stairs creaked under my weight. I reached the landing, surprised she still wasn't there, and half-thought to continue to the kitchen. I even leaned over the railing to see in the direction of the kitchen.

But what was I saying? The darkness brought paranoia, and beside, I was here now facing the knight statue. The answer was at my fingertips.

I flashed the light over the statue. Carved from a white stone, the chess knight stood proudly, nearly the same height as me. The stone was as cool as a rock plucked from the river, polished to a smooth silkiness. The horse's eyes were wide and clear, and his nostrils flared as though in battle. The artist had outdone himself in chiseling this beautiful sculpture.

My fingers trailed over the rock folds that looked like gauze. I touched and felt, searching for some sign of a secret hidden compartment. The statue felt as solid as a mountain.

But I couldn't be wrong. The letters *had* to point here.

Where the heck was Mary? I glanced down again and could barely see the lemony yellow spillage of the kitchen lights warming the far end of the hallway.

"Mary!" I hissed, not wanting to shout.

There was no answer. Then again, I'd been pretty quiet, not wanting to rile Patty. What was she doing?

Suddenly, it made perfect sense that she was fixing herself something to eat. After all, Cook wasn't here. Maybe she was baking a pizza. That took time.

I focused on the statue. Bernie had to have meant the knight, but where? I touched the eyes, smooth like two marbles, and stroked its flowing mane. I traced the muscular neck and then clumsily dropped to my knees. I felt around the square base. Fine filigree decorated the foundation. Sharp edges, beveled at the corners. This sculptor had been a master.

And then I felt it.

The smallest of bumps next to a tiny indent, a pinprick of imperfection. But after taking the time to feel perfection, it stood out like a dead light bulb on a Christmas tree. My fingernail wanted to pick it off, pick it open.

So I tried.

My fingernails scratched against the stone. I tried to dig in, figure it out, pop something open.

I heard a thump behind. "Mary, hurry up! I think I found it."

Suddenly, something clicked under my finger. The steps grew quicker on the floor below me. I flashed my light to the rear of the base, trying to see. Something was about to give. I could feel it. Almost there.

I stooped low, trying to see. Finally, I gave up and stretched out on the landing, my light shining on the base and my fingers extended to reach. There was movement. It was sliding.

I heard her steps on the stairwell now.

"Mary, help me. I found it!"

I could hear her now on the landing. She nudged my leg. I was stuck now, half behind the statue.

"Here, take the phone."

And then a cold feeling washed over me. The nudge had felt heavier than hers should have been. I was stuck, trapped between the stairwell and the stone base. I tried to wiggle out. A hand reached for the phone. It felt smooth. No callouses.

It also was much bigger than mine.

My heart dropped at the trick. The touch felt soft at first. Then it yanked the phone away so hard my hand smashed against the statue.

I crawled out behind the unyielding stone and half rolled to my side.

"No, no. Please continue. You've almost found it, you said?" The crisp accent told me all I needed to know. Gerald had somehow snuck out from the party and now stood before me.

With the light off, I could barely make out his features. Just a glimmer of his teeth. "What did you say about Mary? Is she your friend?"

My mouth dried up like a thousand deserts.

"I don't think she'll be helping you, after all. I think Mary's all tied up."

CHAPTER TWENTY-ONE

The glow of the cellphone highlighted his face in even more shadows. He tossed something at me. It hit my chest with a hard thump.

"Pick it up," he said.

I reached for it and found a chess piece.

"You caught me, you clever girl. You know that, right?"

I stared at him in confusion.

"Back in the library. I saw it in the fireplace and pulled it out."

The object rolled in my hands. I couldn't see it. He must have known that because the light flashed on my hands, highlighting it and covering my hands with a soft white shine.

A chess queen. Exquisitely made and cold as ice.

It was also beautiful.

"Pure white sapphire. Luckily it can withstand some heat."

"This was Bernie's treasure?" I asked, confused.

"This was one of them, although not the one I wanted. The one he told our friend about all those years ago. I tried to get Bernie to show me years ago, but the man was stubborn. I thought you were going to bring it straight to me at the locksmiths. Unfortunately, you brought the picture, not the case."

"How did you know we were going to be there?" I asked the question, but my mind was moving a million miles a minute. Where was Mary? Was she okay? Was she hurt somewhere?

"That darling Patty came and told Janice. Something about Rudy locksmith and an electrical problem? Of course, I was quite intrigued."

"Why are you here? I thought you were at the party with Miss Janice?"

Gerald smirked. "I stepped out for a moment. I'm good at making plausible excuses. It seemed an ideal time to come here and have a look. All quiet-like."

I hated my vulnerable position. I glanced at his ankles to see if they were in reach to kick.

"Be careful with that look on your face," he admonished. "I have a little friend here you don't want to meet." He waved his hand a bit, and something glistened. A pistol.

I glanced away.

"That's better. Now, where were we? Oh, yes. 'Mary, I found it.' So where is it?"

I swallowed hard.

"Well?"

"I'm not sure. Maybe here."

"Find it."

Fear rippled through me. I didn't want to stretch behind the statue again, to expose my rib cage while trapping myself behind the stone.

"Don't force my hand." Gerald shook the pistol. "I'm being quite reasonable here."

My heart galloped, and adrenaline turned my muscles rigid. I jammed my fingers behind the statue again. I still couldn't get the door to open. With my face on the floor, I could see his dress shoes tapping. I tried to stall him. "How did you know about this?"

"I've known about it for years."

"Then why wait until now?"

"I couldn't exactly come back, now could I? Not until everyone who remembered me had gone on to the pearly gates. And maybe I wouldn't have done more than a little snooping. I wasn't too worried. Not until you found Bernie and dug everything all back up again."

The latch wiggled like a loose baby tooth. It felt like it wanted to open. But now I had no idea what would happen if I gave him what he wanted. Would he just kill me?

He tapped me with his foot. "Especially after I heard you talking about something you'd found in the tunnel."

"Where did you hear that?"

"When I was leaving the cigar room, I passed by the kitchen."

"You mean you came and eavesdropped."

Gerald gave a harsh snort. "Of course, I was eavesdropping. You just found the man I murdered. I needed to know what else you guys knew."

It terrified me that he just confessed that. I silently hoped and prayed that Mary would escape and call the police.

He seemed confident that he'd left her incapacitated. By the time she broke free and found a phone, it would probably be too late.

"Hurry up!" he demanded.

"My arm hurts," I complained, hoping he'd buy it.

He wasn't sure if he believed me. I could tell by the squint of his eyes how he weighed my words. But, in the end, he shrugged it off as me being inept. I hoped he'd continue to underestimate me. There was great power in being perceived as weak.

"At any rate, that's what had me go find old butler."

"What?" I wheezed.

He nodded, apparently pleased he'd surprised me. "Yes. I heard you ask about the butler. I knew I'd better get to him first."

CHAPTER TWENTY-TWO

I heard a scuffle from the landing above us, just the slightest sound, like a book falling over. Gerald must have heard it as well because his head jerked up. His eyes narrowed as he searched the darkness. Finally, he blasted the area with his flashlight.

No one was there, plummeting my hopes. It must have been the house creaking. Or, even worse, maybe it was Hank coming to investigate why I'd not returned to bed.

"My arm's going to sleep," I said to distract him.

He placed the heel of his shoe on my ankle, the one I'd twisted in the wall. Slowly he pressed. The pain was immediate, and I bit my tongue to keep from screaming.

"You have two minutes," he said in a tone much lower than before. "Then I'll need to look into ways to persuade you." He eased off.

I closed my eyes. This was it. Time had run out. Stretching a bit, feeling terrifyingly vulnerable, I picked the crack open with my fingernail and reached inside.

There was an envelope in there. It felt reasonably thick. I pulled it out as my shoulder burned from the awkward angle. Once it was free, I rolled to my side and squirmed out. I passed it up to him.

The flashlight swooped over my face.

"I'll be taking that," he said emphatically. He reached down, and his smile grew like the Grinch's.

Just as his fingers touched the paper, I lashed out with my leg as hard as I could. It connected with his knee. The man screamed. Before he could react, I kicked again. And again. Most of them missed, my legs flailed in the air.

Gerald stumbled back to get away. That's what I was hoping for. That was my only chance. Because with his last step back, his foot found nothing but air.

With a startled expression and hands stiffly clawing empty space like a mannequin, Gerald fell down the last flight of stairs.

I climbed to my feet and stepped forward. My ankle's nerves flamed, and I partially collapsed. Lucky for me, my hand made it to the banister or I would have followed after him.

Somewhere down below, Gerald moaned. I searched for my phone where he dropped it. Where was it? I had to call the police!

I couldn't see a thing on the inky landing floor. I dropped to my knees and felt around. It had to be around here somewhere.

Then I heard it, the silence. The creepy stillness that signified something was wrong. I crawled over and stared down the stairwell.

Gerald had managed to stand up. His slicked-back hair now stood atop his head like a parrot's ruff. Slowly, he turned to face me, and my heart rate doubled. His face caught the bit of light from somewhere downstairs and showed itself pale and menacing. Shadows hid his eyes, but I knew he caught sight of me. Or maybe it was my imagination.

"You will pay for that," he snarled.

I rose to my feet, uncertain of what to do. I didn't dare run away, my ankle wouldn't make it. And even if I did manage to escape and hide, he had poor Mary someplace. He could hurt her.

I needed help. Where was my phone?

There was a shuffling noise and then a clump. I glanced back to see him on the first step, although he seemed shaky and hung tight to the railing to pull himself up. By the third step, I could see his strength returning.

"You better be there when I get up, or your friend and I will have to reacquaint ourselves again."

He paused to catch his breath while I swept the floor with my arms, desperate. My fingers brushed something cool and sent it skittering away. The phone! I lunged after it in excitement. The tips of my fingers brushed it before it slid again. This time, I heard another sound, the dismal clatter of the phone slipping through the bannisters and crashing to the hard floor below.

"I'm coming," Gerald growled. His shoes thumped on the treads. Something must've been causing him pain, because he made slow but deliberate progress.

I closed my eyes against the hopeless feeling. All right, girl. Sometimes you have to stand and fight. I grabbed the railing and pulled myself to my feet. I'd kick him again, when he came close, punch him, go for his eyes. I wasn't going to let him get away and hurt someone else.

My hands balled into two fists as I steadied myself. He'd made it halfway up. I couldn't see his face, but his eyes gleamed in the light from the hallway.

I froze. But not because I was ready to meet him. No, it was because I saw a shadow, something even darker than Gerald. It crept up behind him. I swear every hair on my body rose. Was this Bernie's ghost coming for revenge?

Gerald didn't hear the velvety apparition behind him. He had no clue. He grinned, and now I saw his teeth. He thought I had given up.

I swallowed and steadied myself against the railing. My ankle throbbed to remind me not to rely on it.

The man closed the gap, and I saw black streaks running down his face.

Blood.

He was hurt. I could do this. But what would I be facing behind him?

The shape shivered up the stairs. And then I saw it grow in size. It shuddered, and I heard a dull clank. The shape hit Gerald in the head with something that sounded substantial, like Cook's favorite cast iron pan.

Gerald's eyes rolled back in his head. The shape behind him jumped to the side as he collapsed and slid down the stairs, thumping on each step.

Of course, it wasn't a ghost. But who was it? Mary?

The shape turned and smiled. Scary teeth, and not Mary. "Always in trouble, aren't you, Laura Lee?" it said.

And then the jumbled shadows, teeth, and voice all came together, and Patty dropped the frying pan before me.

"We need to call the police," I gasped.

"I've already done that back when I chanced across Mary. I also sent her from the house straight to Mrs. Fitzwater's. I suspect the cavalry will be here soon." She stared down at the still shape slumped at the floor and sniffed. "Not that we'll need them." Then she sighed. "I feel like I have to do everything around here. What would you people do without me?"

CHAPTER TWENTY-THREE

*W*ith her arm around my waist, Patty helped me down the stairs, proving heroes do come in all shapes, sizes, and temperaments. Guilt weighed me down more than my ankle after basically despising her all these weeks.

"Good heavens. You're no feather, are you? Well, that's what happens when you take breaks all the time and eat cookies instead of working."

I stifled my retort. "Thank you, Patty."

We made it to the bottom, where Gerald lay sprawled out. Moments later, loud pounding came from the front entrance, and then the door slammed open, and Stephen appeared, wild-eyed and hair on end. He took one look at me, and then his gaze dropped to Gerald before swinging over to Patty.

"Is there anyone else?" he asked.

"Not that I know. Of course, I came in the middle of this hullabaloo, so ask Laura Lee."

My body trembled like a leaf. "I think it's just him. How are you here?"

"Mary came to my place instead of the neighbors. I left her with Sophia to call the police and came straight away." He gently touched my arm. "You okay?"

His tone alone made my eyes start to puddle. The emotions, the drama, the fear for Mary and myself. I couldn't handle his kindness right now. I nodded and sucked in a deep breath.

He seemed to understand because he gently patted my arm and then examined Gerald. Taking his belt off, Stephen rolled Gerald over and fastened it around the unconscious man's arms.

Patty switched on the foyer chandelier. It blazed, each prism sending slivers of light against the walls and floor. Scattered around us were bits of paper.

Stephen started to gather them up.

"Whoa," he said, examining one.

"What is it?"

He passed it over and then bent to pick up more.

The first picture was of a dead woman. I recognized her. She was the woman in the photo we found in the briefcase, the one with young man David (now known as Gerald). I gasped and covered my mouth. The woman lay behind some trees. It was nighttime, but it was obvious she'd been shot in the chest. The photographer's flash caught all the gruesome details.

The next photo was out of order. It was Gerald fighting with the woman. It appeared they didn't know the picture was being taken, as the photographer used a long lens.

The next photo was more chilling than the first. Gerald had the gun out, and the woman's eyes were wide with shock. The last picture had a blur, as if the photographer had been shaking, but in it Gerald pointed the gun while the woman lay on the ground.

There was a letter that accompanied the photographs.

Nelson

I hardly know who to address this to. I've gone to Terry about my treasure and tried to talk to him about what David did. He would hear nothing of it. I told him I had evidence. Unfortunately, Terry will never forgive me for his family's slight and would not hear me out. Instead, he shouted over me that I owed his father. I feel so alone. I can only hope he won't go straight to David with this news.

But I owe it to our tour guide, Madeline Escott, to let the truth be known. She didn't deserve this and had I known he would stoop to such lengths, I would have stopped him. It was too late. Always too late.

Bernie.

"So that's what Gerald meant," I said, feeling numb.

"What?"

"Gerald said he found out about the treasure from their friend. It was Terry. It was this envelope that Gerald had been searching for all this time. To find the proof that he'd murdered this woman. When he couldn't find it, he murdered Bernie."

Stephen rubbed his neck. "I'm confused. Mary said you figured it was Terry who killed Bernie because of the milkman breaking the window in the door."

"No, that was another crime. When Bernie told Terry about the treasure, naturally, Terry thought it was the real deal. So he thought he'd steal it. In Terry's mind, he was taking back what was their due. Terry talked his dad into hiring Kenner to fix the broken window, when in reality, Terry paid him extra to search the library."

"So the butler didn't know?"

I shook my head. "No. Cook said he was loyal, and I believe her. He had no idea the thoughts his son had, and I'm sure he would have been mortified to have found out."

"What happened to Nelson?"

"Gerald found out we were visiting him and called on him first. Maybe he was afraid butler knew more than he remembered and didn't want him to tip us off. Especially since he was now dating Miss Janice and openly searching for the evidence. After all, he suspected it might be in Janet's room all that while ago."

"It was him in her room?"

I nodded.

"And poor Nelson. What a horrible man. Who would murder someone on their death bed?"

"As you said, a horrible man."

CHAPTER TWENTY-FOUR

"You sure you're ready to go?" Miss Janice stood in the middle of the foyer while Butler held the door open, allowing sunshine to dapple the marble and her sensible square-heeled shoes with warm yellow.

Patty stood in the doorway, her lips pursed and her gaze skittering from Miss Janice to the rest of us acting as a send-off. "I am quite sure. There was a time I thought I could do this place good. But I now see it's too far gone. Dinners at unholy hours, housekeepers with afternoons off, staff disappearing at times at night, not to mention skeletons and holes in the wall. And now this—a murderer allowed in the midst of us. There's only so much a reasonable woman can take. I fear, Miss Janice, we've hit that limit and burst beyond."

I stood there a bit wobbly as Patty made her swan song. My wrapped ankle hurt like the dickens. Normally I wouldn't have even tried to attempt a sad face at her impending departure. However, the woman saved my life and earned my eternal respect and gratitude, and so I plastered on the most regretful expression I could and stiffened my back.

Miss Janice opened her mouth to answer and then snapped it shut again. Finding herself duped by Gerald had put her at a loss for words for the last several days. Instead, she gave a rather humble smile and a dip of her well-coiffed head. "Well, then, I wish you safe journeys."

Patty grabbed her suitcase and turned to the stairs. We all gathered at the entrance and waved goodbye, sounding like a band of professional mourners.

She tottered down the stairs. At the cab she spun around and waved to us as the driver loaded her bags in the trunk. Then she was off.

As the car disappeared through the gates, Miss Janice sighed. She smiled at us, weary and resigned.

"You okay?" Cook asked, patting her arm.

"Tea, Cook, if you please."

Cook nodded sensibly. "I have it ready. Let me take it to your garden room."

"No, I'd rather have it in the kitchen, if that's okay."

"Oh." Cook's eyes went wide.

"I'd prefer some company, if you don't mind."

"Don't mind? Of course! Come on in. This is your kitchen."

Cook declared it was Miss Janice's kitchen, but I knew better. Cook thought this was *her* kitchen, and she was working hard to unbristle and be welcoming to Miss Janice.

"Please, everyone, join me," Miss Janice invited.

We all shot concerned glances at each other, uncertain of what to do.

Mary recovered first. "That would be lovely, thank you."

And so we followed Miss Janice into the kitchen, with Cook leading. Right away, Cook bustled about the kettle, Lucy found more pastries, and Mary and I set out the tea cups.

Miss Janice settled in the seat normally taken by Marguerite. Just seeing her in that spot brought a lump into my throat. What would happen now? Miss Janice would search for a new housekeeper, I was sure. I inwardly groaned at the thought of the adjustment period to a new person. And what if she was worse than Patty?

Meanwhile, poor Miss Janice slumped over her tea cup, her normally proud shoulders curled in an air of defeat. We all noticed and fluttered around to comfort her like a flock of pigeons around a child with bread crumbs.

"It's okay, Miss Janice," Mary murmured.

"He was a bad 'un. Some men are tricky. I'll have you know my sister married a sort just the same. Had kids with him! Imagine that. You've been spared," Cook exclaimed.

Miss Janice brought a weary gaze up at Cook. "I hardly worried about having children. A companion only. And I thought at my age I was more discerning."

Cook clucked her tongue and pushed over a plate of cookies. Feeding grief was what she knew best.

"And to think this was someone Henry once knew as a young man? Mortifying!" Miss Janice collapsed her face into her hands. "I can only imagine what the gossip will be."

We fluttered about as helpless as moths at a porch light, patting her shoulder, pouring more tea, and making sympathetic noises. We were all at a loss for words. If one thing was true, gossip was a silent killer, able to destroy respect and sabotage characters with words that, once released, could never be taken back.

Butler appeared at the doorway then. "Ma'am? Mrs. Fitzwater here to see—"

"Oh, shoo out of the way." The neighbor pushed into the room from behind him. "Janice? Darling, are you okay?"

The beautiful lady glided over with every bit of her actress entrance.

"Clara?" Miss Janice looked up, and I saw her mascara had puddled a bit under her eyes. I ran to get her a tissue.

"Janice! You poor dear! What a scoundrel, and yet your manor is the hero of the town!"

"Wh-what?" Janice sniffled.

"Thornberry Estates! Everyone is talking about it. How you solved not one, but three murders! I assure you, the butcher is crowing from the hilltop on how brave and wonderful you all are. I expect you will be given the key to the city."

"Why?"

"Why? Well you solved his father's murder, that's why. Not to mention poor Bernie Thornberry. And Madeline Escott's siblings plan on giving you the reward. Gerald Hawkings and his son are going away for a very long time."

"His son!" Mary hissed at me. "I wonder if he has a red car!"

I nodded, thinking he probably did. "And met us at Rudy's Locksmith."

"It wasn't me who solved it," Miss Janice said. "It was my girls."

"You do have the best people always surrounding you, that's for sure. Look at you now. You are a lucky woman."

Miss Janice did look then. Tissue in hand, her eyes softened to see how we all encircled her. I smiled, and others did as well.

"We love you, Miss Janice," Mary said.

Her mouth curved a bit at the corners. "Sometimes I forget to count my blessings. Thank you, dear ones. Of course, the reward is all yours."

"I'll enjoy the spot of money, but my reward is Marguerite coming back," Cook huffed.

"Is she?" I asked, as hope surged through me.

Cook nodded vigorously and her cheeks wobbled. "You bet she is. Once Marguerite found out what happened in her absence, she was horrified. As far as she's concerned, this is her home, and no interloper is going to destroy it on her watch."

"And her nephew?" I asked.

"He's moving this way himself. It seems Stephen can help him with a job and Marguerite has an in with a nanny to watch his littles."

"You girls are my heroes," Miss Janice said, her smile growing.

"There was one other hero," I said cautiously.

Miss Janice lifted her eyebrows.

"Hank. He led me to the clues several times. And it was because of him that I first suspected Gerald to begin with."

The women around me froze. Lucy even distanced herself from me. They all knew Miss Janice didn't know the cat still lived here.

The grandfather clock chimed from the foyer and seemed to break the horrid spell we were all under.

Miss Janice breathed, "I hold no fondness for animals and did not realize the cat remained." Her eyes tightened threateningly.

Normally, I'd back down. But not this time. "He's an amazing cat. Without him, I probably wouldn't have suspected a thing and the murders would still be unsolved."

She stared at me still as the clock ticked loudly. Then her gaze darted away. "I remember when Henry came home with him. Pulled him out from under his shirt. The cat was a mess. Skinny as a rail, matted fur, and muddy from the rain. I was horrified he was in the manor. But Henry insisted. He'd found the cat under the overpass and made the driver pull over. That was Henry. He had a soft heart."

"He did indeed," Cook chimed in.

"We had a horrible fight that night," Miss Janice mused. "I think I threw the entry vase."

"Yes, you did," Cook agreed again, animately. "Broke it into a million pieces. I swore it would never get cleaned up."

Mrs. Fitzwater laughed. "Oh, this is getting good. Tell me more."

Miss Janice gave her a smart look. "Of course, Clara. As long as the joke's on me, hm?" And then she smiled. "He took that cat to the veterinarians, and had him all sorted out. Came back and told me that cat's name was Hank. 'Why, Hank?' I'd asked. He said it was for an old storybook character he'd enjoyed as a kid. The cat must have known I didn't care for him because I rarely saw him. He stayed in Henry's study most of the time. Truth be told, I forgot about him after my Henry passed."

As if he knew he was being talked about, Hank entered the kitchen from the pantry.

"Lo, that cat is smart. There he is now," Cook exclaimed.

We all turned to look, each of us expressing some sound of surprise at his uncanny appearance.

Hank blinked at us and then stalked over to Cook and meowed.

"Heavens, I think I forgot to feed him. That's the problem. He's scolding me now," Cook confessed.

Miss Janice watched him with a curious expression. "I used to like cats. I seem to remember I used to like a lot of things that I've since forgotten." She lifted her face to Mrs. Fitzwater. "Was it the passing time that distracted me so much?"

Mrs. Fitzwater shrugged lightly. "It's never too late to get back to your roots," she said. "Like pruning those wild branches on a tree, it's wisdom to learn old habits and thoughts were never going to be fruitful anyway."

Miss Janice nodded as her eyes landed on Hank again. "And he's still wearing that gold collar Henry got him. I swear Henry swiped my bracelet to put the pendant on, although he swore he hadn't. 'You'd never even notice,' he'd told me at the time. 'You have more baubles than a Christmas tree.' Yet I seem to remember he was pretty fond of baubles himself."

We all softly chuckled. The house was a testament to that belief, for sure, with every nook and cranny stuffed with his assorted tchotchkes he'd brought home from his travels.

Miss Janice shocked me then by making a kissing noise to entice him, one that I knew never worked on him. He was too proud to respond to something like that.

Except this time it did. He flicked an ear in her direction and stared, his great green eyes taking her in.

"Here, kitty," she called and lowered her hand. Her fingers looked thin under the rows of gaudy rings.

He started toward her and stopped just out of reach. I held my breath, waiting to see what would happen next.

"I'm sorry, Mr. Hank. I certainly wasn't welcoming when you first showed up, and I haven't been since. That was my fault. Maybe we can learn to be friends, now? For Henry's sake?"

Hank studied her outstretched finger. He slowly walked closer and gave it a sniff. And then he rubbed his cheek against it.

I could have cried.

Miss Janice stroked his cheek. "My goodness, you're so soft." She rubbed his ears gently, and he went back to sniffing her. Then he sat and allowed her to pet him.

I heard it then. I couldn't believe it. Miss Janice did as well and remarked, "Why, I'd forgotten all about cat purrs. And listen to his! He has a mighty purr, like a lion in a cat's body." She stroked his cheek. "Thank you for helping me remember. You're right, Clara. I think it's high time to do a little life pruning. I have a feeling I'm going to discover a lot more."

AFTERWORD

The End

Thank you for reading Catastrophe in the Library. Laura Lee is one of my favorites.

Catch both her and Hank in their continuing story, Poisonous Paws

My other favorite character is Stella O'Neil. Have you had a chance to read the Flamingo Realty Cozy Mysteries? This gal has grown a lot. Her story continues in a brand new mystery, Beach Front Hunt. I am sooo happy for her and her mom!

CPSIA information can be obtained
at www.ICGtesting.com
Printed in the USA
LVHW041651310822
727292LV00005B/52

9 798520 397366